Books by Christopher Isherwood

NOVELS
A Meeting by the River
A Single Man
Down There on a Visit
The World in the Evening
Prater Violet
Goodbye to Berlin
The Last of Mr. Norris
(*English title*: Mr. Norris Changes Trains)
The Memorial
All the Conspirators

AUTOBIOGRAPHY
My Guru and His Disciple
Christopher and His Kind
Kathleen and Frank
Lions and Shadows

BIOGRAPHY
Ramakrishna and His Disciples

PLAYS (*with W. H. Auden*)
On the Frontier
The Ascent of F6
The Dog beneath the Skin

TRAVEL
The Condor and the Cows
Journey to a War (*with W. H. Auden*)

COLLECTION
Exhumations

TRANSLATIONS
The Intimate Journals of Charles Baudelaire
(*and the following with Swami Prabhavananda*)
The Yoga Aphorisms of Patanjali
Shankara's Crest-Jewel of Discrimination
The Bhagavad-Gita

A SINGLE MAN

A

CHRISTOPHER ISHERWOOD

SINGLE

North Point Press
Farrar, Straus and Giroux
New York

MAN

TO
GORE VIDAL

A SINGLE MAN

Waking up begins with saying *am* and *now*. That which has awoken then lies for a while staring up at the ceiling and down into itself until it has recognized *I*, and therefrom deduced *I am, I am now*. *Here* comes next, and is at least negatively reassuring; because *here*, this morning, is where it has expected to find itself: what's called *at home*.

But *now* isn't simply now. *Now* is also a cold reminder: one whole day later than yesterday, one year later than last year. Every *now* is labeled with its date, rendering all past *nows* obsolete, until—later or sooner—perhaps—no, not perhaps—quite certainly: it will come.

Fear tweaks the vagus nerve. A sickish shrinking from what waits, somewhere out there, dead ahead.

But meanwhile the cortex, that grim disciplinarian,

has taken its place at the central controls and has been testing them, one after another: the legs stretch, the lower back is arched, the fingers clench and relax. And now, over the entire intercommunication system, is issued the first general order of the day: UP.

Obediently the body levers itself out of bed—wincing from twinges in the arthritic thumbs and the left knee, mildly nauseated by the pylorus in a state of spasm—and shambles naked into the bathroom, where its bladder is emptied and it is weighed: still a bit over 150 pounds, in spite of all that toiling at the gym! Then to the mirror.

What it sees there isn't so much a face as the expression of a predicament. Here's what it has done to itself, here's the mess it has somehow managed to get itself into during its fifty-eight years; expressed in terms of a dull, harassed stare, a coarsened nose, a mouth dragged down by the corners into a grimace as if at the sourness of its own toxins, cheeks sagging from their anchors of muscle, a throat hanging limp in tiny wrinkled folds. The harassed look is that of a desperately tired swimmer or runner; yet there is no question of stopping. The creature we are watching will struggle on and on until it drops. Not because it is heroic. It can imagine no alternative.

Staring and staring into the mirror, it sees many faces within its face—the face of the child, the boy, the young man, the not-so-young man—all present still, preserved like fossils on superimposed layers, and, like fossils, dead. Their message to this live dying creature is: Look at us—we have died—what is there to be afraid of?

It answers them: But that happened so gradually, so easily. *I'm afraid of being rushed.*

It stares and stares. Its lips part. It starts to breathe through its mouth. Until the cortex orders it impatiently to wash, to shave, to brush its hair. Its nakedness has to be covered. It must be dressed up in clothes because it is going outside, into the world of the other people; and these others must be able to identify it. Its behavior must be acceptable to them.

Obediently, it washes, shaves, brushes its hair, for it accepts its responsibilities to the others. It is even glad that it has its place among them. It knows what is expected of it.

It knows its name. It is called George.

By the time it has gotten dressed, it has become *he;* has become already more or less George —though still not the whole George they demand and are prepared to recognize. Those who call him on the phone at this hour of the morning would be bewildered, maybe even scared, if they could realize what this three-quarters-human thing is that they are talking to. But, of course, they never could—its voice's mimicry of their George is nearly perfect. Even Charlotte is taken in by it. Only two or three times has she sensed something uncanny and asked, "Geo—are you *all right?*"

He crosses the front room, which he calls his study, and comes down the staircase. The stairs turn a corner; they are narrow and steep. You can touch both handrails with your elbows, and you have to bend your head, even if, like George, you are only five eight. This is a tightly planned little house. He often feels protected by its smallness; there is hardly room enough here to feel lonely.

Nevertheless . . .

Think of two people, living together day after day, year after year, in this small space, standing elbow to elbow cooking at the same small stove, squeezing past each other on the narrow stairs, shaving in front of the same small bathroom mirror, constantly jogging, jostling, bumping against each other's bodies by mistake or on purpose, sensually, aggressively, awkwardly, impatiently, in rage or in love—think what deep though invisible tracks they must leave, everywhere, behind them! The doorway into the kitchen has been built too narrow. Two people in a hurry, with plates of food in their hands, are apt to keep colliding here. And it is here, nearly every morning, that George, having reached the bottom of the stairs, has this sensation of suddenly finding himself on an abrupt, brutally broken off, jagged edge—as though the track had disappeared down a landslide. It is here that he stops short and knows, with a sick newness, almost as though it were for the first time: Jim is dead. Is dead.

He stands quite still, silent, or at most uttering a brief animal grunt, as he waits for the spasm to pass. Then he walks into the kitchen. These morning spasms are too painful to be treated sentimentally. After them, he feels relief, merely. It is like getting over a bad attack of cramp.

Today, there are more ants, winding in column across the floor, climbing up over the sink and threatening the closet where he keeps the jams and the honey. Doggedly he destroys them with a Flit gun and has a sudden glimpse of himself doing this: an obstinate, malevolent old thing imposing his will upon these instructive and admirable insects. Life destroying life before an audience of objects— pots and pans, knives and forks, cans and bottles— that have no part in the kingdom of evolution. Why? Why? Is it some cosmic enemy, some arch-tyrant who tries to blind us to his very existence by setting us against our natural allies, the fellow victims of his tyranny? But, alas, by the time George has thought all this, the ants are already dead and mopped up on a wet cloth and rinsed down the sink.

He fixes himself a plate of poached eggs, with bacon and toast and coffee, and sits down to eat them at the kitchen table. And meanwhile, around and around in his head goes the nursery jingle his nanny taught him when he was a child in England, all those years ago:

> *Poached eggs on toast are very nice—*

(He sees her so plainly still, gray-haired with mouse-bright eyes, a plump little body carrying in the nursery breakfast tray, short of breath from climbing all those stairs. She used to grumble at their steepness and call them "The Wooden Mountains"— one of the magic phrases of his childhood.)

> *Poached eggs on toast are very nice,*
> *If you try them once you'll want them twice!*

Ah, the heartbreakingly insecure snugness of those nursery pleasures! Master George enjoying his eggs; Nanny watching him and smiling reassurance that all is safe in their dear tiny doomed world!

Breakfast with Jim used to be one of the best times of their day. It was then, while they were drinking their second and third cups of coffee, that they had their best talks. They talked about everything that came into their heads—including death, of course, and is there survival, and, if so, what exactly is it that survives. They even discussed the relative advantages and disadvantages of getting killed instantly and of knowing you're about to die. But now George can't for the life of him remember what Jim's views were on this. Such questions are hard to take seriously. They seem so academic.

Just suppose that the dead do revisit the living. That something approximately to be described as Jim can return to see how George is making out. Would this be at all satisfactory? Would it even be worth while? At best, surely, it would be like the brief visit of an observer from another country who is permitted to peep in for a moment from the vast outdoors of his freedom and see, at a distance, through glass, this figure who sits solitary at the small table in the narrow room, eating his poached eggs humbly and dully, a prisoner for life.

The living room is dark and low-ceilinged, with bookshelves all along the wall opposite the windows. These books have not made George nobler or better or more truly wise. It is just that he likes listening to their voices, the one or the other, according to his mood. He misuses them quite ruthlessly—despite the respectful way he has to talk about them in public—to put him to sleep, to take his mind off the hands of the clock, to relax the nagging of his pyloric spasm, to gossip him out of his melancholy, to trigger the conditioned reflexes of his colon.

He takes one of them down now, and Ruskin says to him:

. . . you liked pop-guns when you were schoolboys, and rifles and Armstrongs are only the same things better made: but then the worst of it is, that what was play to you when boys, was not play to the sparrows; and what is play to you now, is not play to the small birds of State neither; and for the black eagles, you are somewhat shy of taking shots at them, if I mistake not.

Intolerable old Ruskin, always absolutely in the right, and crazy, and so cross, with his whiskers, scolding the English—he is today's perfect companion for five minutes on the toilet. George feels a bowel movement coming on with agreeable urgency and climbs the stairs briskly to the bathroom, book in hand.

Sitting on the john, he can look out of the window. (They can see his head and shoulders from across the street, but not what he is doing.) It is a gray lukewarm California winter morning; the sky is low and soft with Pacific fog. Down at the shore, ocean and sky will be one soft, sad gray. The palms stand unstirred and the oleander bushes drip moisture from their leaves.

This street is called Camphor Tree Lane. Maybe camphor trees grew here once; there are none now. More probably the name was chosen for its picturesqueness by the pioneer escapists from dingy downtown Los Angeles and stuffy-snobbish Pasadena who came out here and founded this colony back in the early twenties. They referred to their stucco bungalows and clapboard shacks as cottages, giving them cute names like "The Fo'c'sle" and "Hi Nuff." They called their streets lanes, ways or trails, to go with the woodsy atmosphere they wanted to create. Their utopian dream was of a subtropical English village with Montmartre manners: a Little Good Place where you could paint a bit, write a bit, and drink lots. They saw themselves as rear-guard individualists, making a last-ditch stand against the twentieth century. They gave thanks loudly from morn till eve that they had escaped the soul-destroying commercialism of the city. They were tacky and cheerful and defiantly bohemian, tirelessly inquisitive about each other's doings, and boundlessly tolerant. When they fought, at least it was with fists and bottles and furniture, not lawyers. Most of them were lucky enough to have died off before the Great Change.

The Change began in the late forties, when the World War Two vets came swarming out of the East with their just-married wives, in search of new and better breeding grounds in the sunny Southland, which had been their last nostalgic glimpse of home before they shipped out to the Pacific. And what better breeding ground than a hillside neighborhood like this one, only five minutes' walk from the beach and with no through traffic to decimate the future tots? So, one by one, the cottages which used to reek of bathtub gin and reverberate with the poetry of Hart Crane have fallen to the occupying army of Coke-drinking television watchers.

The vets themselves, no doubt, would have adjusted pretty well to the original bohemian utopia; maybe some of them would even have taken to painting or writing between hangovers. But their wives explained to them, right from the start and in the very clearest language, that breeding and bohemianism do not mix. For breeding you need a steady job, you need a mortgage, you need credit, you need insurance. And don't you dare die, either, until the family's future is provided for.

So the tots appeared, litter after litter after litter. And the small old schoolhouse became a group of big new airy buildings. And the shabby market on the ocean front was enlarged into a super. And on Camphor Tree Lane two signs were posted. One of them told you not to eat the watercress which grew along the bed of the creek, because the water was polluted. (The original colonists had been eating it for years; and George and Jim tried some and it tasted delicious and nothing happened.) The other sign—those sinister black silhouettes on a yellow ground—said CHILDREN AT PLAY.

George and Jim saw the yellow sign, of course, the first time they came down here, house-hunting. But they ignored it, for they had already fallen in love with the house. They loved it because you could only get to it by the bridge across the creek; the surrounding trees and the steep bushy cliff behind shut it in like a house in a forest clearing. "As good as being on our own island," George said. They waded ankle-deep in dead leaves from the sycamore (a chronic nuisance); determined, now, to like everything. Peering into the low damp dark living room, they agreed how cozy it would be at night with a fire. The garage was covered with a vast humped growth of ivy, half dead, half alive, which made it twice as big as itself; inside it was tiny, having been built in the days of the model T Ford. Jim thought it would be useful for keeping some of the animals in. Their cars were both too big for it, anyway, but they could be parked on the bridge. The bridge was beginning to sag a little, they noticed. "Oh well, I expect it'll last our time," said Jim.

No doubt the neighborhood children see the house very much as George and Jim saw it that first afternoon. Shaggy with ivy and dark and secret-looking, it is just the lair you'd choose for a mean old storybook monster. This is the role George has found himself playing, with increasing violence, since he started to live alone. It releases a part of his nature which he hated to let Jim see. What would Jim say if he could see George waving his arms and roaring like a madman from the window, as Mrs. Strunk's Benny and Mrs. Garfein's Joe dash back and forth across the bridge on a dare? (Jim always got along with them so easily. He would let them pet the skunks and the raccoon and talk to the myna bird; and yet they never crossed the bridge without being invited.)

Mrs. Strunk, who lives opposite, dutifully scolds her children from time to time, telling them to leave him alone, explaining that he's a professor and has to work so hard. But Mrs. Strunk, sweet-natured though she is—grown wearily gentle from toiling around the house at her chores, gently melancholy from regretting her singing days on radio; all given up in order to bear Mr. Strunk five boys and two girls—even she can't refrain from telling George, with a smile of motherly indulgence and just the faintest hint of approval, that Benny (her youngest) now refers to him as "That Man," since George ran Benny clear out of the yard, across the bridge and down the street; he had been beating on the door of the house with a hammer.

George is ashamed of his roarings because they aren't playacting. He does genuinely lose his temper and feels humiliated and sick to his stomach later. At

21

the same time, he is quite well aware that the children want him to behave in this way. They are actually willing him to do it. If he should suddenly refuse to play the monster, and they could no longer provoke him, they would have to look around for a substitute. The question Is this playacting or does he really hate us? never occurs to them. They are utterly indifferent to him except as a character in their myths. It is only George who cares. Therefore he is all the more ashamed of his moment of weakness about a month ago, when he bought some candy and offered it to a bunch of them on the street. They took it without thanks, looking at him curiously and uneasily; learning from him maybe at that moment their first lesson in contempt.

Meanwhile, Ruskin has completely lost his wig. "Taste is the ONLY morality!" he yells, wagging his finger at George. He is getting tiresome, so George cuts him off in midsentence by closing the book. Still sitting on the john, George looks out of the window.

The morning is quiet. Nearly all the kids are in

school; the Christmas vacation is still a couple of weeks away. (At the thought of Christmas, George feels a chill of desperation. Maybe he'll do something drastic, take a plane to Mexico City and be drunk for a week and run wild around the bars. *You won't, and you never will,* a voice says, coldly bored with him.)

Ah, here's Benny, hammer in hand. He hunts among the trash cans set out ready for collection on the sidewalk and drags out a broken bathroom scale. As George watches, Benny begins smashing it with his hammer, uttering cries as he does so; he is making believe that the machine is screaming with pain. And to think that Mrs. Strunk, the proud mother of this creature, used to ask Jim, with shudders of disgust, how he could bear to touch those harmless baby king snakes!

And now out comes Mrs. Strunk onto her porch, just as Benny completes the murder of the scale and stands looking down at its scattered insides. "Put them back!" she tells him. "Back in the can! Put them back, now! Back! Put them back! Back in the can!" Her voice rises, falls, in a consciously sweet singsong. She never yells at her children. She has read all the psychology books. She knows that Benny is passing through his Aggressive Phase, right on schedule; it just couldn't be more normal and healthy. She is well aware that she can be heard clear down the street. It is her right to be heard, for this is the Mothers' Hour. When Benny finally drops some of the broken parts back into the trash can, she singsongs "Attaboy!" and goes back smiling into the house.

23

So Benny wanders off to interfere with three much smaller tots, two boys and a girl, who are trying to dig a hole on the vacant lot between the Strunks and the Garfeins. (Their two houses face the street frontally, wide-openly, in apt contrast to the sidewise privacy of George's lair.)

On the vacant lot, under the huge old eucalyptus tree, Benny has taken over the digging. He strips off his windbreaker and tosses it to the little girl to hold; then he spits on his hands and picks up the spade. He is someone or other on TV, hunting for buried treasure. These tot-lives are nothing but a medley of such imitations. And soon as they can speak, they start trying to chant the singing commercials.

But now one of the boys—perhaps because Benny's digging bores him in the same way that Mr. Strunk's scoutmasterish projects bore Benny—strolls off by himself, firing a carbide cannon. George has been over to see Mrs. Strunk about this cannon, pleading with her to please explain to the boy's mother that it is driving him slowly crazy. But Mrs. Strunk has no intention of interfering with the anarchy of nature. Smiling evasively, she tells George, "*I* never hear the noise children make—just as long as it's a *happy* noise."

Mrs. Strunk's hour and the power of motherhood will last until midafternoon, when the big boys and girls return from school. They arrive in mixed groups —from which nearly all of the boys break away at once, however, to take part in the masculine hour of the ball-playing. They shout loudly and harshly to

24

each other, and kick and leap and catch with arrogant grace. When the ball lands in a yard, they trample flowers, scramble over rock gardens, burst into patios without even a thought of apology. If a car ventures along the street, it must stop and wait until they are ready to let it through; they know their rights. And now the mothers must keep their tots indoors out of harm's way. The girls sit out on the porches, giggling together. Their eyes are always on the boys, and they will do the weirdest things to attract their attention: for example, the Cody daughters keep fanning their ancient black poodle as though it were Cleopatra on the Nile. They are disregarded, nevertheless, even by their own boy friends; for this is not their hour. The only boys who will talk to them now are soft-spoken and gentle, like the doctor's pretty sissy son, who ties ribbons to the poodle's curls.

And then, at length, the men will come home from their jobs. And it is their hour; and the ball-playing must stop. For Mr. Strunk's nerves have not been improved by trying all day long to sell that piece of real estate to a butterfly-brained rich widow, and Mr. Garfein's temper is uncertain after the tensions of his swimming-pool installation company. They and their fellow fathers can bear no more noise. (On Sundays Mr. Strunk will play ball with his sons, but this is just another of his physical education projects, polite and serious and no real fun.)

Every weekend there are parties. The teen-agers are encouraged to go off and dance and pet with each other, even if they haven't finished their homework;

25

for the grownups need desperately to relax, unob-
served. And now Mrs. Strunk prepares salads with
Mrs. Garfein in the kitchen, and Mr. Strunk gets the
barbecue going on the patio, and Mr. Garfein, crossing the vacant lot with a tray of bottles and a shaker,
announces joyfully, in Marine Corps tones, "Mar-
toonies coming up!"

And two, three hours later, after the cocktails and
the guffaws, the quite astonishingly dirty stories, the
more or less concealed pinching of other wives' fan-
nies, the steaks and the pie, while The Girls—as Mrs.
Strunk and the rest will continue to call themselves
and each other if they live to be ninety—are washing
up, you will hear Mr. Strunk and his fellow husbands
laughing and talking on the porch, drinks in hand,
with thickened speech. Their business problems are
forgotten now. And they are proud and glad. For
even the least among them is a co-owner of the American utopia, the kingdom of the good life upon earth
—crudely aped by the Russians, hated by the Chinese
—who are nonetheless ready to purge and starve
themselves for generations, in the hopeless hope of
inheriting it. Oh yes indeed, Mr. Strunk and Mr. Garfein are proud of their kingdom. But why, then, are
their voices like the voices of boys calling to each
other as they explore a dark unknown cave, growing
ever louder and louder, bolder and bolder? Do they
know that they are afraid? No. But they are very
afraid.

What are they afraid of?

They are afraid of what they know is somewhere in

the darkness around them, of what may at any moment emerge into the undeniable light of their flashlamps, nevermore to be ignored, explained away. The fiend that won't fit into their statistics, the Gorgon that refuses their plastic surgery, the vampire drinking blood with tactless uncultured slurps, the bad-smelling beast that doesn't use their deodorants, the unspeakable that insists, despite all their shushing, on speaking its name.

Among many other kinds of monster, George says, they are afraid of little me.

Mr. Strunk, George supposes, tries to nail him down with a word. *Queer,* he doubtless growls. But, since this is after all the year 1962, even he may be expected to add, I don't give a damn what he does just as long as he stays away from me. Even psychologists disagree as to the conclusions which may be reached about the Mr. Strunks of this world, on the basis of such a remark. The fact remains that Mr. Strunk himself, to judge from a photograph of him taken in football uniform at college, used to be what many would call a living doll.

But Mrs. Strunk, George feels sure, takes leave to differ gently from her husband; for she is trained in the new tolerance, the technique of annihilation by blandness. Out comes her psychology book—bell and candle are no longer necessary. Reading from it in sweet singsong she proceeds to exorcise the unspeakable out of George. No reason for disgust, she intones, no cause for condemnation. Nothing here that is willfully vicious. All is due to heredity, early environment

27

(Shame on those possessive mothers, those sex-segregated British schools!), arrested development at puberty, and-or glands. Here we have a misfit, debarred forever from the best things of life, to be pitied, not blamed. Some cases, caught young enough, *may* respond to therapy. As for the rest—ah, it's so sad; especially when it happens, as let's face it it does, to truly worthwhile people, people who might have had so much to offer. (Even when they are geniuses in spite of it, their masterpieces are invariably *warped.*) So let us be understanding, shall we, and remember that, after all, there *were* the Greeks (though that was a bit different, because they were pagans rather than neurotics). Let us even go so far as to say that this kind of relationship can sometimes be almost beautiful—particularly if one of the parties is already dead, or, better yet, both.

How dearly Mrs. Strunk would enjoy being sad about Jim! But, aha, she doesn't know; none of them know. It happened in Ohio, and the L.A. papers didn't carry the story. George has simply spread it around that Jim's folks, who are getting along in years, have been trying to persuade him to come back home and live with them; and that now, as the result of his recent visit to them, he will be remaining in the East indefinitely. Which is the gospel truth. As for the animals, those devilish reminders, George had to get them out of his sight immediately; he couldn't even bear to think of them being anywhere in the neighborhood. So, when Mrs. Garfein wanted to know if he would sell the myna bird, he answered that he'd shipped them all back to Jim. A dealer from San Diego took them away.

And now, in reply to the questions of Mrs. Strunk and the others, George answers that, yes indeed, he has just heard from Jim and that Jim is fine. They ask him less and less often. They are inquisitive but quite incurious, really.

But your book is wrong, Mrs. Strunk, says George, when it tells you that Jim is the substitute I found for a real son, a real kid brother, a real husband, a real wife. Jim wasn't a substitute for anything. And there is no substitute for Jim, if you'll forgive my saying so, anywhere.

Your exorcism has failed, dear Mrs. Strunk, says George, squatting on the toilet and peeping forth from his lair to watch her emptying the dustbag of her vacuum cleaner into the trash can. The unspeakable is still here—right in your very midst.

Damnation. The phone.

Even with the longest cord the phone company will give you, it won't reach into the bathroom. George gets himself off the seat and shuffles into the study, like a man in a sack race.

"Hello."

"Hello—is that—it *is* you, Geo?"

"Hello, Charley."

"I say, I didn't call too early, did I?"

"No." (Oh dear, she has managed to get him irritated already! Yet how can he reasonably blame her for the discomfort of standing nastily unwiped, with his pants around his ankles? One must admit, though, that Charlotte has a positively clairvoyant knack of picking the wrong moment to call.)

"You're sure?"

"Of course I'm sure. I've already had breakfast."

"I was afraid if I waited any longer you'd have gone off to the college. . . . My goodness, I hadn't noticed it was *so* late! Oughtn't you to have started already?"

"This is the day I have only one class. It doesn't begin until eleven thirty. My early days are Mondays and Wednesdays." (All this is explained in a tone of slightly emphasized patience.)

"Oh yes—yes, of course! How stupid of me! I *always* forget."

(A silence. George knows she wants to ask him something. But he won't help her. He is rubbed the wrong way by her blunderings. *Why* does she imply that she *ought* to know his college schedule? Just more of her possessiveness. Then why, if she really thinks she ought to know it, does she get it all mixed up?)

"Geo—" (very humbly) "would you *possibly* be free tonight?"

"Afraid not. No." (One second before speaking he couldn't have told you what he was going to answer. It's the desperation in Charlotte's voice that decides him. He isn't in the mood for one of her crises.)

"Oh—I see. . . . I was afraid you wouldn't be. It *is* short notice, I know." (She sounds half stunned, very quiet, hopeless. He stands there listening for a sob. None can be heard. His face is puckered into a grimace of guilt and discomfort—the latter caused by his increasing awareness of stickiness and trussed ankles.)

"I suppose you couldn't—I mean—I suppose it's something important?"

"I'm afraid it is." (The grimace of guilt relaxes. He is mad at her now. He won't be nagged at.)

"I see. . . . Oh well, never mind." (She's brave, now.) "I'll try you again, may I, in a few days?"

"Of course." (Oh—why not be a little nicer, now she's been put in her place?) "Or I'll call you."

(A pause.)

"Well—goodbye, Geo."

"Goodbye, Charley."

Twenty minutes later, Mrs. Strunk, out on her porch watering the hibiscus bushes, watches him back his car out across the bridge. (It is sagging badly nowadays. She hopes he will have it fixed; one of the children might get hurt.) As he makes the half-turn onto the street, she waves to him. He waves to her.

Poor man, she thinks, living there all alone. He has a kind face.

It is one of the marvels and blessings of the Los Angeles freeway system that you can now get from the beach to San Tomas State College in fifty minutes, give or take five, instead of the nearly two hours you would have spent, in the slow old days, crawling from stop light to stop light clear across the downtown area and out into the suburbs beyond.

George feels a kind of patriotism for the freeways. He is proud that they are so fast, that people get lost on them and even sometimes panic and have to bolt for safety down the nearest cutoff. George loves the freeways because he can still cope with them; because the fact that he can cope proves his claim to be a functioning member of society. He can still *get by*.

(Like everyone with an acute criminal complex, George is hyperconscious of all bylaws, city ordinances, rules and petty regulations. Think of how many Public Enemies have been caught just because they neglected to pay a parking ticket! Never once has he seen his passport stamped at a frontier, his driver's license accepted by a post-office clerk as evidence of identity, without whispering gleefully to himself, *Idiots—fooled them again!*)

He will fool them again this morning, in there, in the midst of the mad metropolitan chariot race— Ben-Hur would certainly chicken out—jockeying from lane to lane with the best of them, never dropping below eighty in the fast left lane, never getting rattled when a crazy teen-ager hangs on to his tail or a woman (it all comes of letting them go first through doorways) cuts in sharply ahead of him. The cops on their motorcycles will detect nothing, yet, to warn them to roar in pursuit flashing their red

33

lights, to signal him off to the side, out of the running, and thence to escort him kindly but ever so firmly to some beautifully ordered nursery-community where Senior Citizens ("old," in our country of the bland, has become nearly as dirty a word as "kike" or "nigger") are eased into senility, retaught their childhood games but with a difference: it's known as "passive recreation" now. Oh, by all means let them screw, if they can still cut the mustard; and, if they can't, let them indulge without inhibitions in babylike erotic play. Let them get married, even—at eighty, at ninety, at a hundred—who cares? Anything to keep them busy and stop them wandering around blocking the traffic.

There's always a slightly unpleasant moment when you drive up the ramp which leads onto the freeway and become what's called "merging traffic." George has that nerve-crawling sensation which can't be removed by simply checking the rearview mirror: that, inexplicably, invisibly, he's about to be hit in the back. And then, next moment, he has merged and is away, out in the clear, climbing the long, easy gradient toward the top of the pass and the Valley beyond.

And now, as he drives, it is as if some kind of auto-hypnosis exerts itself. We see the face relax, the shoulders unhunch themselves, the body ease itself back into the seat. The reflexes are taking over; the left foot comes down with firm, even pressure on the clutch pedal, while the right prudently feeds in gas. The left hand is light on the wheel; the right slips the gearshift with precision into high. The eyes, moving unhurriedly from road to mirror, mirror to road, calmly measure the distances ahead, behind, to the nearest car. . . . After all, this is no mad chariot race—that's only how it seems to onlookers or nervous novices—it is a river, sweeping in full flood toward its outlet with a soothing power. There is nothing to fear, as long as you let yourself go with it; indeed, you discover, in the midst of its stream-speed, a sense of indolence and ease.

And now something new starts happening to George. The face is becoming tense again, the muscles bulge slightly at the jaw, the mouth tightens and twitches, the lips are pressed together in a grim line, there is a nervous contraction between the eyebrows. And yet, while all this is going on, the rest of the body remains in a posture of perfect relaxation. More and more it appears to separate itself, to become a separate entity: an impassive anonymous chauffeur-figure with little will or individuality of its own, the very embodiment of muscular co-ordination, lack of anxiety, tactful silence, driving its master to work.

And George, like a master who has entrusted the driving of his car to a servant, is now free to direct his attention elsewhere. As they sweep over the crest of the pass, he is becoming less and less aware of externals—the cars all around, the dip of the freeway ahead, the Valley with its homes and gardens opening below, under a long brown smear of smog, beyond and above which the big barren mountains rise. He has gone deep down inside himself.

What is he up to?

On the edge of the beach, a huge, insolent highrise building which will contain one hundred apartments is growing up within its girders; it will block the view along the coast from the park on the cliffs above. A spokesman for this project says, in answer to objections, Well, that's progress. And anyhow, he implies, if there are people who are prepared to pay $450 a month for this view by renting our apartments, why should you park-users (and that includes George) get it for free?

A local newspaper editor has started a campaign against sex deviates (by which he means people like George). They are everywhere, he says; you can't go into a bar any more, or a men's room, or a public library, without seeing hideous sights. And they all, without exception, have syphilis. The existing laws against them, he says, are far too lenient.

A senator has recently made a speech, declaring

that we should attack Cuba right now, with everything we've got, lest the Monroe Doctrine be held
cheap and of no account. The senator does not deny
that this will probably mean rocket war. We must
face this fact; the alternative is dishonor. We must
be prepared to sacrifice three quarters of our population (including George).

It would be amusing, George thinks, to sneak into
that apartment building at night, just before the
tenants moved in, and spray all the walls of all the
rooms with a specially prepared odorant which
would be scarcely noticeable at first but which would
gradually grow in strength until it reeked like rotting
corpses. They would try to get rid of it with every
deodorant known to science, but in vain; and when
they had finally, in desperation, ripped out the plas-
ter and woodwork, they would find that the girders
themselves were stinking. They would abandon the
place as the Khmers did Angkor; but its stink would
grow and grow until you could smell it clear up the
coast to Malibu. So at last the entire structure would
have to be taken apart by workers in gas masks and
ground to powder and dumped far out in the ocean.
. . . Or perhaps it would be more practical to discover a kind of virus which would eat away whatever
it is that makes metal hard. The advantage that this
would have over the odorant would be that only a
single injection in one spot would be necessary, for
the virus would then eat through all the metal in the
building. And then, when everybody had moved in
and while a big housewarming party was in progress,

37

the whole thing would sag and subside into a limp tangled heap, like spaghetti.

Then, that newspaper editor, George thinks, how funny to kidnap him and the staff-writers responsible for the sex-deviate articles—and maybe also the police chief, and the head of the vice squad, and those ministers who endorsed the campaign from their pulpits—and take them all to a secret underground movie studio where, after a little persuasion—no doubt just showing them the red-hot pokers and pincers would be quite sufficient—they would perform every possible sexual act, in pairs and in groups, with a display of the utmost enjoyment. The film would then be developed and prints of it would be rushed to all the movie theaters. George's assistants would chloroform the ushers so the lights couldn't be turned up, lock the exits, overpower the projectionists, and proceed to run the film under the heading of Coming Attractions.

And as for that senator, wouldn't it be rather amusing to . . .

No.

(At this point, we see the eyebrows contract in a more than usually violent spasm, the mouth thin to knife-blade grimness.)

No. Amusing is *not* the word. These people are not amusing. They should never be dealt with amusingly. They understand only one language: brute force.

Therefore we must launch a campaign of systematic terror. In order to be effective, this will require an organization of at least five hundred highly skilled killers and torturers, all dedicated individuals. The head of the organization will draw up a list of clearly defined, simple objectives, such as the removal of that apartment building, the suppression of that newspaper, the retirement of that senator. They will then be dealt with in order, regardless of the time taken or the number of casualties. In each case, the principal criminal will first receive a polite note, signed "Uncle George," explaining exactly what he must do before a certain deadline if he wants to stay alive. It will also be explained to him that Uncle George operates on the theory of guilt by association.

One minute after the deadline, the killing will begin. The execution of the principal criminal will be delayed for some weeks or months, to give him opportunity for reflection. Meanwhile, there will be daily reminders. His wife may be kidnaped, garroted, embalmed and seated in the living room to await his return from the office. His children's heads may arrive in cartons by mail, or tapes of the screams his relatives utter as they are tortured to death. His friend's homes may be blown up in the night. Anyone who has ever known him will be in mortal danger.

When the organization's 100 per cent efficiency has been demonstrated a sufficient number of times, the population will slowly begin to learn that Uncle George's will must be obeyed instantly and without question.

But does Uncle George *want* to be obeyed? Doesn't he prefer to be defied so he can go on killing and killing—since all these people are just vermin and the more of them that die the better? All are, in the last analysis, responsible for Jim's death; their words, their thoughts, their whole way of life willed it, even though they never knew he existed. But, when George gets in as deep as this, Jim hardly matters any more. Jim is nothing now but an excuse for hating three quarters of the population of America. . . . George's jaws work, his teeth grind, as he chews and chews the cud of his hate.

But does George really hate all these people? Aren't they themselves merely an excuse for hating? What *is* George's hate, then? A stimulant, nothing more; though very bad for him, no doubt. Rage, resentment, spleen—of such is the vitality of middle age. If we say that he is quite crazy at this particular moment, then so, probably, are at least half a dozen others in these many cars around him, all slowing now as the traffic thickens, going downhill, under the bridge, up again past the Union Depot. . . . God! Here we are, downtown already! George comes up dazed to the surface, realizing with a shock that the chauffeur-figure has broken a record: never before has it managed to get them this far entirely on its own. And this raises a disturbing question: Is the chauffeur steadily becoming more and more of an individual? Is it getting ready to take over much larger areas of George's life?

No time to worry about that now. In ten minutes they will have arrived on campus. In ten minutes,

George will have to be George—the George they have named and will recognize. So now he consciously applies himself to thinking their thoughts, getting into their mood. With the skill of a veteran he rapidly puts on the psychological make-up for this role he must play.

No sooner have you turned off the freeway onto San Tomas Avenue than you are back in the tacky sleepy slowpoke Los Angeles of the thirties, still convalescent from the depression, with no money to spare for fresh coats of paint. And how charming it is! An up-and-down terrain of steep little hills with white houses of cracked stucco perched insecurely on their sides and tops, it is made to look quaint rather than ugly by the mad, hopelessly intertwisted cat's cradle of wires and telephone poles. Mexicans live here, so there are lots of flowers. Negroes live here, so it is cheerful. George would not care to live here, because they all blast all day long with their radios and television sets. But he would never find himself yelling at their children, because these peo-

41

ple are not The Enemy. If they would ever accept George, they might even be allies. They never figure in the Uncle George fantasies.

The San Tomas State College campus is back on the other side of the freeway. You cross over to it by a bridge, back into the nowadays of destruction-recon-struction-destruction. Here the little hills have been trucked away bodily or had their tops sliced off by bulldozers, and the landscape is gashed with raw terraces. Tract upon tract of low-roofed dormitory-dwellings (invariably called "homes" and described as "a new concept in living") are being opened up as fast as they can be connected with the sewers and the power lines. It is a slander to say that they are identical; some have brown roofs, some green, and the tiles in their bathrooms come in several different colors. The tracts have their individuality, too. Each one has a different name, of the kind that realtors can always be relied on to invent: Sky Acres, Vista Grande, Grovenor Heights.

The storm center of all this grading, shoveling, hauling and hammering is the college campus itself. A clean modern factory, brick and glass and big windows, already three-quarters built, is being finished in a hysterical hurry. (The contruction noises are such that in some classrooms the professors can hardly be heard.) When the factory is fully operational, it will be able to process twenty thousand graduates. But, in less than ten years, it will have to cope with forty or fifty thousand. So then everything will be torn down again and built up twice as tall.

However, it is arguable that by that time the campus will be cut off from the outside world by its own parking lots, which will then form an impenetrable forest of cars abandoned in despair by the students during the week-long traffic jams of the near future. Even now, the lots are half as big as the campus itself and so full that you have to drive around from one to another in search of a last little space. Today George is lucky. There is room for him on the lot nearest his classroom. George slips his parking card into the slot (thereby offering a piece of circumstantial evidence that he *is* George); the barrier rises in spastic, mechanical jerks, and he drives in.

George has been trying to train himself, lately, to recognize his student's cars. (He is continually starting these self-improvement projects: sometimes it's memory training, sometimes a new diet, sometimes just a vow to read some unreadable Hundredth Best Book. He seldom perseveres in any of them for long.) Today he is pleased to be able to spot three cars—not counting the auto scooter which the Italian exchange student, with a courage or provincialism bordering on insanity, rides up and down the freeway as though he were on the Via Veneto. There's the beat-up, not-so-white Ford coupe belonging to Tom Kugelman, on the back of which he has printed SLOW WHITE. There's the Chinese-Hawaiian boy's grime-gray Pontiac, with one of those joke-stickers in the rear window: THE ONLY ISM I BELIEVE IN IS ABSTRACT EXPRESSIONISM. The joke isn't a joke in his particular case, because he really is an abstract painter. (Or is this some supersubtlety?) At all events, it seems incongruous that anyone with such a sweet Chessy-cat smile and cream-smooth skin and cat-clean neatness could produce such gloomy muddy canvases or own such a filthy car. He has the beautiful name of Alexander Mong. And there's the well-waxed, spotless scarlet MG driven by Buddy Sorensen, the wild watery-eyed albino who is a basketball star and wears a "Ban the Bomb" button. George has caught glimpses of Buddy streaking past on the freeway, laughing to himself as if the absurd little sitzbath of a thing had run away with him and he didn't care.

So now George has arrived. He is not nervous in the least. As he gets out of his car, he feels an upsurge of energy, of eagerness for the play to begin. And he walks eagerly, with a springy step, along the gravel path past the Music Building toward the Department office. He is all actor now—an actor on his way up from the dressing room, hastening through the backstage world of props and lamps and stagehands to make his entrance. A veteran, calm and assured, he pauses for a well-measured moment in the doorway of the office and then, boldly, clearly, with the subtly modulated British intonation which his public demands of him, speaks his opening line: "Good morning!"

And the three secretaries—each one of them a charming and accomplished actress in her own chosen style—recognize him instantly, without even a flicker of doubt, and reply "Good morning!" to him. (There is something religious here, like responses in

44

church—a reaffirmation of faith in the basic American dogma that it is, always, a *good* morning. Good, despite the Russians and their rockets, and all the ills and worries of the flesh. For of course we know, don't we, that the Russians and the worries are not really real? They can be un-thought and made to vanish. And therefore the morning can be made to be good. Very well then, it *is* good.)

Every teacher in the English Department has his or her pigeonhole in this office, and all of them are stuffed with papers. What a mania for communication! A notice of the least important committee meeting on the most trivial of subjects will be run off and distributed in hundreds of copies. Everybody is informed of everything. George glances through all his papers and then tosses the lot into the wastebasket, with one exception: an oblong card slotted and slitted and ciphered by an IBM machine, expressing some poor bastard of a student's academic identity. Indeed, this card *is* his identity. Suppose, instead of signing it as requested and returning it to the Personnel office, George were to tear it up? Instantly, that student would cease to exist, as far as San Tomas State was concerned. He would become academically invisible and only reappear with the very greatest difficulty, after performing the most elaborate propitiation ceremonies: countless offerings of forms filled out in triplicate and notarized affidavits to the gods of the IBM.

George signs the card, holding it steady with two fingertips. He dislikes even to touch these things, for

they are the runes of an idiotic but nevertheless po-
tent and evil magic: the magic of the think-machine
gods, whose cult has one dogma, *We cannot make a
mistake*. Their magic consists in this: that whenever
they do make a mistake, which is quite often, it is
perpetuated and thereby becomes a non-mistake. . . .
Carrying the card by its extreme corner, George brings
it over to one of the secretaries, who will see that it
gets back to Personnel. The secretary has a nail file
on her desk. George picks it up, saying, "Let's see if
that old robot'll know the difference," and pretends to
be about to punch another slit in the card. The girl
laughs, but only after a split-second look of sheer terror; and the laugh itself is forced. George has uttered
blasphemy.

Feeling rather pleased with himself, he leaves the
Department building, headed for the cafeteria.

He starts across the largish open space which is the
midst of the campus, surrounded by the Art Building, the gymnasium, the Science Building and the
Administration Building, and newly planted with
grass and some hopeful little trees which should make
it leafy and shadowy and pleasant within a few years:
that is to say, about the time when they start tearing
the whole place apart again. The air has a tang of
smog—called "eye irritation" in blandese. The mountains of the San Gabriel Range—which still give San
Tomas State something of the glamour of a college
high on a plateau of the Andes, on the few days you
can see them properly—are hidden today as usual in

the sick yellow fumes which arise from the metropolitan mess below.

And now, all around George, approaching him, crossing his path from every direction, is the male and female raw material which is fed daily into this factory, along the conveyer belts of the freeways, to be processed, packaged and placed on the market: Negroes, Mexicans, Jews, Japanese, Chinese, Latins, Slavs, Nordics, the dark heads far predominating over the blond. Hurrying in pursuit of their schedules, loitering in flirty talk, strolling in earnest argument, muttering some lesson to themselves alone—all book-burdened, all harassed.

What do they think they're up to, here? Well, there is the official answer: preparing themselves for life which means a job and security in which to raise children to prepare themselves for life which means a job and security in which. But, despite all the vocational advisers, the pamphlets pointing out to them what good money you can earn if you invest in some solid technical training—pharmacology, let's say, or accountancy, or the varied opportunities offered by the vast field of electronics—there are still, incredibly enough, quite a few of them who persist in writing poems, novels, plays! Goofy from lack of sleep, they scribble in snatched moments between classes, part-time employment and their married lives. Their brains are dizzy with words as they mop out an operating room, sort mail at a post office, fix baby's bottle, fry hamburgers. And somewhere, in the midst of their servitude to the must-be, the mad might-be whispers to them to live, know, experience—what? *Marvels!* The Season in Hell, the Journey to the End of the Night, the Seven Pillars of Wisdom, the Clear Light of the Void. . . . Will any of them make it? Oh, sure. One, at least. Two or three at most—in all these searching thousands.

Here, in their midst, George feels a sort of vertigo. Oh God, what will become of them all? What chance have they? Ought I to yell out to them, right now, here, that it's hopeless?

But George knows he can't do that. Because, absurdly, inadequately, in spite of himself, almost, he is a representative of the hope. And the hope is not false. No. It's just that George is like a man trying to sell a real diamond for a nickel, on the street. The diamond is protected from all but the tiniest few, because the great hurrying majority can never stop to dare to believe that it could conceivably be real.

Outside the cafeteria are announcements of the current student activities: Squaws' Night, Golden Fleece Picnic, Fogcutters' Ball, Civic Society Meeting and the big game against LPSC. These advertised rituals of the San Tomas Tribe aren't quite convincing; they are promoted only by a minority of eager beavers. The rest of these boys and girls do not really think of themselves as a tribe, although they are willing to pretend that they do on special occasions. All that they actually have in common is their urgency: the need to get with it, to finish that assignment which should have been handed in three days ago.

48

When George eavesdrops on their conversation, it is nearly always about what they have failed to do, what they fear the professor will make them do, what they have risked not doing and gotten away with.

The cafeteria is crammed. George stands at the door, looking around. Now that he is a public utility, the property of STSC, he is impatient to be used. He hates to see even one minute of himself being wasted. He starts to walk among the tables with a tentative smile, a forty-watt smile ready to be switched up to a hundred and fifty watts just as soon as anyone asks for it.

Now, to his relief, he sees Russ Dreyer, and Dreyer rises from his table to greet him. He has no doubt been on the lookout for George. Dreyer has gradually become George's personal attendant, executive officer, bodyguard. He is an angular, thin-faced young man with a flat-top haircut and rimless glasses. He wears a somewhat sporty Hawaiian shirt which, on him, seems like a prim shy concession to the sportiness of the clothes around him. His undershirt, appearing in the open V of his unbuttoned collar, looks surgically clean, as always. Dreyer is a grade A scholar, and his European counterpart would probably be a rather dry and brittle stick. But Dreyer is neither dry nor brittle. He has discreet humor and, as an ex-Marine, considerable toughness. He once described to George a typical evening he and his wife, Marinette, spent with his buddy Tom Kugelman and Tom's wife. "Tom and I got into an argument about *Finnegan's Wake*. It went on all through supper. So then the girls said they were sick of listening to us, so they went out to a movie. Tom and I did the dishes and it got to be ten o'clock and we were still arguing and we hadn't convinced each other. So we got some beer out of the icebox and went out in the yard. Tom's building a shed there, but he hasn't got the roof on yet. So then he challenged me to a chinning match, and we started chinning ourselves on the crossbeam over the door, and I whipped him thirteen to eleven."

George is charmed by this story. Somehow, it's like classical Greece.

"Good morning, Russ."

"Good morning, sir." It isn't the age difference which makes Dreyer call George "sir." As soon as they come to the end of this quasi-military relationship, he will start saying "George," or even "Geo," without hesitation.

Together they go over to the coffee machine, fill mugs, select doughnuts from the counter. As they turn toward the cash desk, Dreyer slips ahead of George with the change ready. "No—let me, sir."

"You're always paying."

Dreyer grins. "We're in the chips, since I put Marinette to work."

"She got that teaching job?"

"It just came through. Of course, it's only temporary. The only snag is, she has to get up an hour earlier."

"So you're fixing your own breakfast?"

"Oh, I can manage. Till she gets a job nearer in.

Or I get her pregnant." He visibly enjoys this man-to-man stuff with George. (Does he know about me? George wonders; do any of them? Oh yes, probably. It wouldn't interest them. They don't want to know about my feelings or my glands or anything below my neck. I could just as well be a severed head carried into the classroom to lecture to them from a dish.)

"Say, that reminds me," Dreyer is saying, "Marinette wanted me to ask you, sir—we were wondering if you could manage to get out to us again before too long? We could cook up some spaghetti. And maybe Tom could bring over that tape I was telling you about—the one he got from the audio-visual up at Berkeley, of Katherine Anne Porter reading her stuff—"

"That'd be fine," says George vaguely, with enthusiasm. He glances up at the clock. "I say, we ought to be going."

Dreyer isn't in the least damped by his vagueness. Probably he does not want George to come to supper any more than George wants to go. It is all, all symbolic. Marinette has told him to ask, and he has asked, and now it is on record that George has accepted, for the second time, an invitation to their home. And this means that George is an intimate and can be referred to in after years as part of their circle in the old days. Oh yes, the Dreyers will loyally do their part to make George's place secure among the grand old bores of yesteryear. George can just picture one of those evenings in the 1990's, when Russ is dean of an English department in the Middle West and Marinette is the mother of grown-up sons and daughters. An audience of young instructors and their wives, symbolically entertaining Dr. and Mrs. Dreyer, will be symbolically thrilled to catch the Dean in an anecdotal mood, mooning and mumbling with a fuddled smile through a maze of wowless sagas, into which George and many many others will enter, uttering misquotes. And Marinette, permanently smiling, will sit listening with the third ear—the one that has heard it all before—and praying for eleven o'clock to come. And it will come. And all will agree that this has been a memorable evening indeed.

As they walk toward the classroom, Dreyer asks George what he thinks about what Dr. Leavis said about Sir Charles Snow. (These far-off unhappy Old Things and their long ago battles are still hot news out here in Sleepy Hollow State.) "Well, first of all—" George begins.

They are passing the tennis courts at this moment. Only one court is occupied, by two young men playing singles. The sun has come out with sudden fierce heat through the smog-haze, and the two are stripped nearly naked. They have nothing on their bodies but gym shoes and thick sweatsocks and knit shorts of the kind cyclists wear, very short and close-fitting, molding themselves to the buttocks and the loins. They are absolutely unaware of the passers-by, isolated in the intentness of their game. You would think there was no net between them. Their nakedness makes them seem close to each other and directly opposed, body to body, like fighters. If this were a fight, though, it would be one-sided, for the boy on the left is much the smaller. He is Mexican, maybe, black-haired, handsome, catlike, cruel, compact, lithe, muscular, quick and graceful on his feet. His body is a natural dark gold-brown; there is a fuzz of curly black hair on his chest and belly and thighs. He plays hard and fast, with cruel mastery, baring his white teeth, unsmiling, as he slams back the ball. He is going to win. His opponent, the big blond boy, already knows this; there is a touching gallantry in his defense. He is so sweet-naturedly beautiful, so nobly made; and yet his classical cream-marble body seems a handicap to him. The rules of the game inhibit it from functioning. He is fighting at a hopeless disadvantage. He should throw away his useless racket, vault over the net, and force the cruel little gold cat to submit to his marble strength. No, on the contrary, the blond boy accepts the rules, binds himself by them, will suffer defeat and humiliation rather than break them. His helpless bigness and blondness give him an air of unmodern chivalry. He will fight clean, a perfect sportsman, until he has lost the last game. And won't this keep happening to him all through his life? Won't he keep getting himself involved in the wrong kind of game, the kind of game he was never born to play, against an opponent who is quick and clever and merciless?

This game is cruel; but its cruelty is sensual and stirs George into hot excitement. He feels a thrill of pleasure to find the senses so eager in their response;

53

too often, now, they seem sadly jaded. From his heart, he thanks these young animals for their beauty. And they will never know what they have done to make this moment marvelous to him, and life itself less hateful. . . .

Dreyer is saying, "Sorry, sir—I lost you for a minute, there. I understand about the two cultures, of course —but do you mean you *agree* with Dr. Leavis?" Far from taking the faintest interest in the tennis players, Dreyer walks with his body half turned away from them, his whole concentration fixed upon George's talking head.

For it obviously *has* been talking. George realizes this with the same discomfiture he felt on the freeway, when the chauffeur-figure got them clear downtown. Oh yes, he knows from experience what the talking head can do, late in the evening, when he is bored and tired and drunk, to help him through a dull party. It can play back all of George's favorite theories—just as long as it isn't argued with; then it may become confused. It knows at least three dozen of his best anecdotes. But *here,* in broad daylight, during campus hours, when George should be on-stage every second, in full control of his performance! Can it be that talking head and the chauffeur are in league? *Are they maybe planning a merger?*

"We really haven't time to go into all this right now," he tells Dreyer smoothly. "And anyhow, I'd like to check up on the Leavis lecture again. I've still got that issue of *The Spectator* somewhere at home, I think. . . . Oh, by the way, did you ever get to read that piece on Mailer, about a month ago—in *Esquire*, wasn't it? It's one of the best things I've seen in a long time. . . ."

George's classroom has two doors in its long side wall, one up front, the other at the back of the room. Most of the students enter from the back because, with an infuriating sheep-obstinacy, they love to huddle together, confronting their teachers from behind a barricade of empty seats. But this semester the class is only a trifle smaller than the capacity of the room. Late-comers are forced to sit farther and farther forward, to George's sly satisfaction; finally, they have to take the second row. As for the front row, which most of them shun so doggedly, George can fill that up with his regulars: Russ Dreyer, Tom Kugelman, Sister Maria, Mr. Stoessel, Mrs. Netta Torres, Kenny Potter, Lois Yamaguchi.

George never enters the classroom with Dreyer, or any other student. A deeply rooted dramatic instinct forbids him to do so. This is really all that he uses his office for—as a place to withdraw into before class, simply in order to re-emerge from it and make his entrance. He doesn't interview students in it, because these offices are shared by at least two faculty members, and Dr. Gottlieb, who teaches the Metaphysical Poets, is nearly always there. George cannot talk to another human being as if the two of them were alone when, in fact, they aren't. Even such a harmless question as "What do you *honestly* think of Emerson?" sounds indecently intimate, and such a mild criticism as "What you've written is a mixed metaphor and it doesn't mean anything" sounds unnecessarily cruel, when Dr. Gottlieb is right there at the other desk listening or, what's worse, pretending not to listen. But Gottlieb obviously doesn't feel this way. Perhaps it is a peculiarly British scruple.

So now, leaving Dreyer, George goes into the office. It is right across the hallway. Gottlieb isn't there, for a wonder. George peeps out of the window between the slats of the Venetian blinds and sees, in the far distance, the two tennis players still at their game. He coughs, fingers the telephone directory without looking at it, closes the empty drawer in his desk, which has been pulled open a little. Then, abruptly, he turns, takes his briefcase out of the closet, leaves the office and crosses to the front classroom door.

His entrance is quite undramatic according to conventional standards. Nevertheless, this is a subtly contrived, outrageously theatrical effect. No hush falls as George walks in. Most of the students go right on talking. But they are all watching him, waiting for him to give some sign, no matter how slight, that the class is to begin. The effect is a subtle but gradually increasing tension, caused by George's teasing refusal to give this sign and the students' counterdetermination not to stop talking until he gives it.

Meanwhile, he stands there. Slowly, deliberately, like a magician, he takes a single book out of his briefcase and places it on the reading desk. As he does this, his eyes move over the faces of the class. His lips curve in a faint but bold smile. Some of them smile back at him. George finds this frank confrontation extraordinarily exhilarating. He draws strength from these smiles, these bright young eyes. For him, this is one of the peak moments of the day. He feels brilliant, vital, challenging, slightly mysterious and, above all, *foreign*. His neat dark clothes, his white dress shirt and tie (the only tie in the room) are uncompromisingly alien from the aggressively virile informality of the young male students. Most of these wear sneakers and garterless white wool socks, jeans in cold weather, and in warm weather shorts (the thigh-clinging Bermuda type—the more becoming short ones aren't considered quite decent). If it is really warm, they'll roll up their sleeves and sometimes leave their shirts provocatively unbuttoned to show curly chest hair and a St. Christopher medal. They look as if they were ready at any minute to switch from studying to ditchdigging or gang fighting. They seem like mere clumsy kids in contrast with the girls, for these have all outgrown their teenage phase of Capri pants, sloppy shirts and giant heads of teased-up hair. They are mature women, and

57

they come to class dressed as if for a highly respectable party.

This morning George notes that all of his front-row regulars are present. Dreyer and Kugelman are the only ones he has actually asked to help fill the gap by sitting there; the rest of them have their individual reasons for doing so. While George is teaching, Dreyer watches him with an encouraging alertness; but George knows that Dreyer isn't really impressed by him. To Dreyer, George will always remain an academic amateur; his degrees and background are British and therefore dubious. Still, George is the Skipper, the Old Man; and Dreyer, by supporting his authority, supports the structure of values up which he himself proposes to climb. So he wills George to be brilliant and impress the outsiders—that is to say, everyone else in the class. The funny thing is that Dreyer, with the clear conscience of absolute loyalty, feels free to whisper to Kugelman, *his* lieutenant, as often as he wants to. Whenever this happens, George longs to stop talking and listen to what they are saying about him. Instinctively, George is sure that Dreyer would never dream of talking about anyone else during class: *that* would be bad manners.

Sister Maria belongs to a teaching order. Soon she'll get her credential and become a teacher herself. She is, no doubt, a fairly normal, unimaginative, hard-working good young woman; and no doubt she sits up front because it helps her concentrate, maybe even because the boys still interest her a little and she wants to avoid looking at them. But we, most of us, lose our sense of proportion in the presence of a nun; and George, thus exposed at short range to this bride of Christ in her uncompromising medieval habit, finds himself becoming flustered, defensive. An unwilling conscript in Hell's legions, he faces the soldier of Heaven across the front line of an exceedingly polite cold war. In every sentence he addresses to her, he calls her "Sister"; which is probably just what she doesn't want.

Mr. Stoessel sits in the front row because he is deaf and middle-aged and only lately arrived from Europe, and his English is terrible.

Mrs. Netta Torres is also middle-aged. She seems to be taking this course out of mere curiosity or to fill in idle hours. She has the look of a divorcee. She sits up front because her interest is centered frankly and brutally on George as George. She watches rather than listens to him. She even seems to be "reading" his words indirectly, through a sort of Braille made up of his gestures, inflections, mannerisms. And this almost tactile scrutiny is accompanied by a motherly smile, for, to Mrs. Torres, George is just a small boy, really, and so cute. George would love to catch her out and discourage her from attending his class by giving her low grades. But, alas, he can't. Mrs. Torres is listening as well as watching; she can repeat what he has been saying, word for word.

Kenny Potter sits in the front row because he's what's nowadays called crazy, meaning only that he tends to do the opposite of what most people do; not on principle, however, and certainly not out of aggressiveness. Probably he's too vague to notice the manners and customs of the tribe, and too lazy to follow them, anyway. He is a tall skinny boy with very broad stooped shoulders, gold-red hair, a small head, small bright-blue eyes. He would be conventionally handsome if he didn't have a beaky nose; but it is a nice one, a large, humorous organ.

George finds himself almost continuously aware of Kenny's presence in the room, but this doesn't mean that he regards Kenny as an ally. Oh, no—he can never venture to take Kenny for granted. Sometimes when George makes a joke and Kenny laughs his deep, rather wild, laugh, George feels he is being laughed with. At other times, when the laugh comes a fraction of a moment late, George gets a spooky impression that Kenny is laughing not at the joke but at the whole situation: the educational system of this country, and all the economic and political and psychological forces which have brought them into this classroom together. At such times, George suspects Kenny of understanding the innermost meaning of life—of being, in fact, some sort of a genius (though you would certainly never guess this from his term papers). And then again, maybe Kenny is just very young for his age, and misleadingly charming, and silly.

Lois Yamaguchi sits beside Kenny because she is his girl friend; at least, they are nearly always together. She smiles at George in a way that makes him wonder if she and Kenny have private jokes about him—but who can be sure of anything with these enigmatic Asians? Alexander Mong smiles enigmatically, too, though his beautiful head almost certainly contains nothing but clotted oil paint. Lois and Alexander are by far the most beautiful creatures in the class; their beauty is like the beauty of plants, seemingly untroubled by vanity, anxiety or effort.

All this while, the tension has been mounting. George has continued to smile at the talkers and to preserve his wonderful provocative melodramatic silence. And now, at last, after nearly four whole minutes, his silence has conquered them. The talking dies down. Those who have already stopped talking shush the others. George has triumphed. But his triumph lasts only for a moment. For now he must break his own spell. Now he must cast off his mysteriousness and stand revealed as that dime-a-dozen thing, a teacher, to whom the class has got to listen, no matter whether he drools or stammers or speaks with the tongue of an angel—that's neither here nor there. The class has got to listen to George because, by virtue of the powers vested in him by the State of California, he can make them submit to and study even his crassest prejudices, his most irresponsible caprices, as so many valuable clues to the problem: How can I impress, flatter or otherwise con this cantankerous old thing into giving me a good grade?

Yes, alas, now he must spoil everything. Now he must speak.

After many a summer *dies* the swan.' "

George rolls the words off his tongue with such hammy harmonics, such shameless relish, that this sounds like a parody of W. B. Yeats reciting. (He comes down on "dies" with a great thump to compensate for the "And" which Aldous Huxley has chopped off from the beginning of the original line.) Then, having managed to startle or embarrass at least a few of them, he looks around the room with an ironical grin and says quietly, schoolmasterishly, "I take it you've all read the Huxley novel by this time, seeing that I asked you to more than three weeks ago?"

Out of the corner of his eye, he notices Buddy Sorensen's evident dismay, which is not unexpected, and Estelle Oxford's indignant *now*-they-tell-me shrug of the shoulders, which is more serious. Estelle is one of his brightest students. Just because she is bright, she is more conscious of being a Negro, apparently, than the other colored students in the class are; in fact, she is hypersensitive. George suspects her of suspecting him of all kinds of subtle discrimination. Probably she wasn't in the room when he told them to read the novel. Damn, he should have noticed that and told her later. He is a bit intimidated by her. Also he likes her and is sorry. Also he resents the way she makes him feel.

"Oh well," he says, as nicely as he can, "if any of you haven't read it yet, that's not too important. Just listen to what's said this morning, and then you can read it and see if you agree or disagree."

He looks at Estelle and smiles. She smiles back. So, this time, it's going to be all right.

"The title is, of course, a quotation from Tennyson's poem 'Tithonus.' And, by the way, while we're on the subject—who *was* Tithonus?"

Silence. He looks from face to face. Nobody knows. Even Dreyer doesn't know. And, Christ, how typical this is! Tithonus doesn't concern them because he's at two removes from their subject. Huxley, Tennyson, Tithonus. They're prepared to go as far as Tennyson, but not one step farther. There their curiosity ends. Because, basically, *they don't give a shit.* . . .

"You *seriously* mean to tell me that none of you know who Tithonus was? That none of you could be bothered to find out? Well then, I advise you *all* to spend part of your weekend reading Grave's *Greek Myths, and* the poem itself. I must say, I don't see how anyone can pretend to be interested in a novel when he doesn't even stop to ask himself what its title means."

This spurt of ill temper dismays George as soon as he has discharged it. Oh dear, he *is* getting nasty!

63

And the worst is, he never knows when he's going to behave like this. He has no time to check himself. Shamefaced now, and avoiding all their eyes—Kenny Potter's particularly—he fastens his gaze high up on the wall opposite.

"Well, to begin at the beginning, Aphrodite once caught her lover Ares in bed with Eos, the goddess of the Dawn. (You'd better look them *all* up, while you're about it.) Aphrodite was furious, of course, so she cursed Eos with a craze for handsome mortal boys —to teach her to leave other people's gods alone." (George gets a giggle on this line from someone and is relieved; he has feared they would be offended by their scolding and would sulk.) Not lowering his eyes yet, he continues, with a grin sounding in his voice, "Eos was terribly embarrassed, but she found she just couldn't control herself, so she started kidnaping and seducing boys from the earth. Tithonus was one of them. As a matter of fact, she took his brother Ganymede along too—for company—" (Louder giggles, from several parts of the room, this time.) "Unfortunately, Zeus saw Ganymede and fell madly in love with him." (If Sister Maria is shocked, that's too bad. George doesn't look at her, however, but at Wally Bryant—about whom he couldn't be more certain— and, sure enough, Wally is wriggling with delight.) "So, knowing that she'd have to give up Ganymede anyway, Eos asked Zeus, wouldn't he, in exchange, make Tithonus immortal? So Zeus said, of course, why not? And he did it. But Eos was so stupid, she forgot to ask him to give Tithonus eternal youth as

64

well. Incidently, that could quite easily have been arranged; Selene, the Moon goddess, fixed it up for her boy friend Endymion. The only trouble there was that Selene didn't care to do anything but kiss, whereas Endymion had other ideas; so she put him into an eternal sleep to keep him quiet. And it's not much fun being beautiful for ever and ever, when you can't even wake up and look at yourself in a mirror." (Nearly everybody is smiling, now—yes, even Sister Maria. George beams at them. He does so hate unpleasantness.) "Where was I? Oh yes—so poor Tithonus gradually became a repulsively immortal old man—" (Loud laughter.) "And Eos, with the characteristic heartlessness of a goddess, got bored with him and locked him up. And he got more and more gaga, and his voice got shriller and shriller, until suddenly one day he turned into a cicada."

This is a miserably weak payoff. George hasn't expected it to work, and it doesn't. Mr. Stoessel is quite frantic with incomprehension and appeals to Dreyer in desperate whispers. Dreyer whispers back explanations, which cause further misunderstandings. Mr. Stoessel gets it at last and exclaims, "ach so—*eine Zikade!*" in a reproachful tone which implies that it's George and the entire Anglo-American world who have been mispronouncing the word. But by now George has started up again—and with a change of attitude. He's no longer wooing them, entertaining them; he's telling them, briskly, authoritatively. It is the voice of a judge, summing up and charging the jury.

"Huxley's general reason for choosing this title is obvious. However, you will have to ask yourselves how far it will bear application in detail to the circumstances of the story. For example, the fifth Earl of Gonister can be accepted as a counterpart of Tithonus, and he ends by turning into a monkey, just as Tithonus turned into an insect. But what about Jo Stoyte? And Dr. Obispo? He's far more like Goethe's Mephistopheles than like Zeus. And who is Eos? Not Virginia Maunciple, surely. For one thing, I feel sure she doesn't get up early enough." Nobody sees this joke. George still sometimes throws one away, despite all his experience, by muttering it, English style. A bit piqued by their failure to applaud, he continues, in an almost bullying tone, "But, before we can go any further, you've got to make up your minds what this novel actually *is* about."

They spend the rest of the hour making up their minds.

At first, as always, there is blank silence. The class sits staring, as it were, at the semantically prodigious word. *About. What is it about?* Well, what does George want them to say it's about? They'll say it's about anything he likes, anything at all. For nearly all of them, despite their academic training, deep, deep down still regard this *about* business as a tiresomely sophisticated game. As for the minority who have cultivated the *about* approach until it has become second nature, who dream of writing an *about* book of their own one day, on Faulkner, James or Conrad, proving definitively that all previous *about*

66

books on that subject are about nothing—they aren't
going to say anything yet awhile. They are waiting
for the moment when they can come forward like
star detectives with the solution to Huxley's crime.
Meanwhile, let the little ones flounder. Let the mud
be stirred up, first.

The mud is obligingly stirred up by Alexander
Mong. He knows what he's doing, of course. He isn't
dumb. Maybe it's even part of his philosophy as an
abstract painter to regard anything figurative as
merely childish. A Caucasian would get aggressive
about this, but not Alexander. With that beautiful
Chinese smile, he says, "It's about this rich guy who's
jealous because he's afraid he's too old for this girl
of his, and he thinks this young guy is on the make
for her, only he isn't, and he doesn't have a hope,
because she and the doctor already made the scene.
So the rich guy shoots the young guy by mistake, and
the doctor like covers up for them and then they all
go to England to find this Earl character who's
monkeying around with a chick in a cellar—"

A roar of joy at this. George smiles good-sportingly
and says, "you left out Mr. Pordage and Mr. Propter
—what do they do?"

"Pordage? Oh yes—he's the one that finds out about
the Earl eating those crazy fish—"

"Carp."

"That's right. And Propter—" Alexander grins and
scratches his head, clowning it up a bit—"I'm sorry,
sir. You'll just have to excuse me. I mean, I didn't hit
the sack till like half past two this morning, trying

67

to figure that cat out. Wow! I don't dig that jazz."

More laughter. Alexander has fulfilled his function. He has put the case, charmingly, for the philistines. Now tongues are loosened and the inquest can proceed.

Here are some of its findings:

Mr. Propter shouldn't have said the ego is unreal; this proves that he has no faith in human nature.

This novel is arid and abstract mysticism. What do we need eternity for, anyway?

This novel is clever but cynical. Huxley should dwell more on the warm human emotions.

This novel is a wonderful spiritual sermon. It teaches us that we aren't meant to pry into the mysteries of life. We mustn't tamper with eternity.

Huxley is marvelously zany. He wants to get rid of people and make the world safe for animals and spirits.

To say time is evil because evil happens in time is like saying the ocean is a fish because fish happen in the ocean.

Mr. Propter has no sex life. This makes him unconvincing as a character.

Mr. Pordage's sex life is unconvincing.

Mr. Propter is a Jeffersonian democrat, an anarchist, a bolshevik, a proto-John-Bircher.

Mr. Propter is an escapist. This is illustrated by the conversation with Pete about the Civil War in Spain. Pete was a good guy until Mr. Propter brainwashed him and he had a failure of nerve and started to believe in God.

Huxley really understands women. Giving Virginia a rose-colored motor scooter was a perfect touch.

And so on and so forth. . . .

George stands there smiling, saying very little, letting them enjoy themselves. He presides over the novel like an attendant at a carnival booth, encouraging the crowd to throw and smash their targets; it's all good clean fun. However, there are certain ground rules which must be upheld. When someone starts in about mescaline and lysergic acid, implying that Mr. Huxley is next door to being a dope addict, George curtly contradicts him. When someone else coyly tries to turn the *clef* in the *roman*—Is there, couldn't there be some connection between a certain notorious lady and Jo Stoyte's shooting of Pete?— George tells him absolutely not; *that* fairytale was exploded back in the thirties.

And now comes a question George has been expecting. It is asked, of course, by Myron Hirsch, that indefatigable heckler of the *goyim*. "Sir, here on page seventy-nine, Mr. Propter says the stupidest text in the Bible is '*they hated me without a cause.*' Does he mean by that the Nazis were right to hate the Jews? Is Huxley antisemitic?"

George draws a long breath. "No," he answers mildly.

And then, after a pause of expectant silence—the

class is rather thrilled by Myron's bluntness—he repeats, loudly and severely, "No—Mr. Huxley it *not* antisemitic. The Nazis were *not* right to hate the Jews. But their hating the Jews was *not* without a cause. No one *ever* hates without a cause. . . .

"Look—let's leave the Jews out of this, shall we? Whatever attittude you take, it's impossible to discuss Jews objectively nowadays. It probably won't be possible for the next twenty years. So let's think about this in terms of some other minority, any one you like, but a small one—one that isn't organized and doesn't have any committees to defend it. . . ."

George looks at Wally Bryant with a deep shining look that says, I am with you, little minority-sister. Wally is plump and sallow-faced, and the care he takes to comb his wavy hair and keep his nails filed and polished and his eyebrows discreetly plucked only makes him that much less appetizing. Obviously he has understood George's look. He is embarrassed. Never mind! George is going to teach him a lesson now that he'll never forget. Is going to turn Wally's eyes into his timid soul. Is going to give him courage to throw away his nail file and face the truth of his life. . . .

"Now, for example, people with freckles aren't thought of as a minority by the non-freckled. They *aren't* a minority in the sense we're talking about. And why aren't they? Because a minority is only thought of as a minority when it constitutes some kind of a threat to the majority, real or imaginary. And no threat is ever *quite* imaginary. Anyone here

70

disagree with that? If you do, just ask yourself, What would this particular minority do if it suddenly became the majority overnight? You see what I mean? Well, if you don't—think it over!

"All right. Now along come the liberals—including everybody in this room, I trust—and they say, 'Minorities are just people, like us.' Sure, minorities are people—*people*, not angels. Sure, they're like us—but not *exactly* like us; that's the all-too-familiar state of liberal hysteria in which you begin to kid yourself you honestly cannot see any difference between a Negro and a Swede. . . ." (Why, oh why daren't George say "between Estelle Oxford and Buddy Sorensen"? Maybe, if he did dare, there would be a great atomic blast of laughter, and everybody would embrace, and the kingdom of heaven would begin, right here in classroom 278. But then again, maybe it wouldn't.)

"So, let's face it, minorities are people who probably look and act and think differently from us and have faults we don't have. We may dislike the way they look and act, and we may hate their faults. And it's *better* if we admit to disliking and hating them than if we try to smear our feelings over with pseudo-liberal sentimentality. If we're frank about our feelings, we have a safety valve; and if we have a safety valve, we're actually less likely to start persecuting. I know that theory is unfashionable nowadays. We all keep trying to believe that if we ignore something long enough it'll just vanish. . . .

"Where was I? Oh yes. Well, now, suppose this

71

minority does get persecuted, never mind why—
political, economic, psychological reasons. There always *is* a reason, no matter how wrong it is—that's
my point. And, of course, persecution itself it always
wrong; I'm sure we all agree there. But the worst of
it is, we now run into another liberal heresy. *Because*
the persecuting majority is vile, says the liberal,
therefore the persecuted minority must be stainlessly
pure. Can't you see what nonsense that is? What's to
prevent the bad from being persecuted by the worse?
Did all the Christian victims in the arena have to be
saints?

"And I'll tell you something else. A minority has
its own kind of aggression. It absolutely dares the
majority to attack it. It hates the majority—not without a cause, I grant you. It even hates the other
minorities, because all minorities are in competition:
each one proclaims that its sufferings are the worst
and its wrongs are the blackest. And the more they
all hate, and the more they're all persecuted, the nas-
tier they become! Do you think it makes people nasty
to be loved? You know it doesn't! Then why should
it make them nice to be loathed? While you're being
persecuted, you hate what's happening to you, you
hate the people who are making it happen; you're
in a world of hate. Why, you wouldn't recognize love
if you met it! You'd suspect love! You'd think there
was something behind it—some motive—some trick.
. . ."

By this time, George no longer knows what he has
proved or disproved, whose side, if any, he is arguing

on, or indeed just exactly what he is talking about. And yet these sentences have blurted themselves out of his mouth with genuine passion. He has meant every one of them, be they sense or nonsense. He has administered them like strokes of a lash, to whip Wally awake, and Estelle too, and Myron, and all of them. He who has ears to hear, let him hear. . . .

Wally continues to look embarrassed—but, no, neither whipped nor awakened. And now George becomes aware that Wally's eyes are no longer on his face; they are raised and focused on a point somewhere behind him, on the wall above his head. And now, as he glances rapidly across the room, faltering, losing momentum, George sees all the other pairs of eyes raised also—focused on that damned clock. He doesn't need to turn and look for himself; he knows he must be running overtime. Brusquely he breaks off, telling them, "We'll go on with this on Monday." And they all rise instantly to their feet, collecting their books, breaking into chatter.

Well, after all, what else can you expect? They have to hurry, most of them, to get someplace else within the next ten minutes. Nevertheless, George's feathers are ruffled. It's been a long time since last he forgot and let himself get up steam like this, right at the end of a period. How humiliating! The silly enthusiastic old prof, rambling on, disregarding the clock, and the class sighing to itself, He's off again! Just for a moment, George hates them, hates their brute basic indifference, as they drain quickly out of the room. Once again, the diamond has been offered publicly for a nickel, and they have turned from it with a shrug and a grin, thinking the old peddler crazy.

So he smiles with an extra benevolence on the three who have lingered behind to ask him questions. But Sister Maria merely wants to know if George, when he sets the final examination, will require them to have read all of those books which Mr. Huxley mentions in this novel. George thinks, How amusing to tell her, yes, including *The 120 Days of Sodom*. But he doesn't, of course. He reassures her and she goes away happy, her academic load that much lighter.

And then Buddy Sorensen merely wants to excuse himself. "I'm sorry, sir. I didn't read the Huxley because I thought you'd be going through it with us first." Is this sheer idiocy or slyness? George can't be bothered to find out. "Ban the Bomb!" he says, looking at Buddy's button; and Buddy, to whom he has said this before, grins happily. "Yes, sir, you bet!"

Mrs. Netta Torres wants to know if Mr. Huxley had an actual English village in mind as the original of his Gonister. George is unable to answer this. He can only tell Mrs. Torres that, in the last chapter, when Obispo and Stoyte and Virginia are in search of the fifth Earl, they appear to be driving out of London in a southwesterly direction. So, most likely, Gonister is supposed to be somewhere in Hampshire or Sussex. . . . But now it becomes clear that Mrs. Torres' question has been a pretext, merely. She has brought up the subject of England in order to tell him that she spent three unforgettable weeks there, ten years ago. Only most of it was in Scotland, and the rest all in London. "Whenever you're speaking to us," she tells George, as her eyes fervently probe his face, "I keep remembering that beautiful accent. It's like music." (George is strongly tempted to ask her just which accent she has in mind. Can it be Cockney or Gorbals?) And now Mrs. Torres wants to know the name of his birthplace, and he tells her, and she has never heard of it. He takes advantage of her momentary frustration to break off their *tête-à-tête*.

Again George's office comes in useful; he goes into it to escape from Mrs. Torres. He finds Dr. Gottlieb there.

Gottlieb is all excited because he has just received from England a new book about Francis Quarles, written by an Oxford don. Gottlieb probably knows every bit as much about Quarles as the don does. But Oxford, towering up in all its majesty behind this don, its child, utterly overawes poor little Gottlieb, who was born in one of the wrong parts of Chicago. "It makes you realize," he says, "the background you need, to do a job like this." And George feels saddened and depressed, because Gottlieb obviously wishes, above all else in life, that he could turn himself into that miserable don and learn to write his spiteful-playful, tight-assed vinegar prose.

Having held the book in his hands for a moment and turned its pages with appropriate respect, George decides that he needs something to eat. As he steps out of the building, the first people he recognizes are Kenny Potter and Lois Yamaguchi. They are sitting on the grass under one of the newly planted trees. Their tree is even smaller than the others. It has barely a dozen leaves on it. To sit under it at all seems ridiculous; perhaps this is just why Kenny chose it. He and Lois look as though they were children playing at being stranded on a South Pacific atoll. Thinking this, George smiles at them. They smile back, and then Lois starts to laugh, in her dainty-shamefaced Japanese way. George passes quite close by their atoll as a steamship might, without stopping. Lois seems to know what he is, for she waves gaily to him exactly as one waves to a steamship, with an enchantingly delicate gesture of her tiny wrist and hand. Kenny waves also, but it is doubtful if *he* knows; he is only following Lois's example. Anyhow, their waving charms George's heart. He waves back to them. The old steamship and the young castaways have exchanged signals—but not signals for help. They respect each other's privacy. They have no desire for involvement. They simply wish each other well. Again, as by the tennis players, George feels that his day has been brightened; but, this time, the emotion isn't in the least disturbing. It is peaceful, radiant. George steams on toward the cafeteria, smiling to himself, not even wanting to look back.

But then he hears "Sir!" right behind him, and he turns and it's Kenny. Kenny has come running up silently in his sneakers. George supposes he will ask some specific question such as what book are they going to read next in class, and then leave again. But no, Kenny drops into step beside him, remarking in a matter-of-fact voice, "I have to go down to the bookshop." He doesn't ask if George is going to the book shop and George doesn't tell him that he hasn't been planning to.

"Did you ever take mescaline, sir?"

"Yes, once. In New York. That was about eight years ago. There weren't any regulations against selling it then. I just went into a drugstore and ordered some. They'd never heard of it, but they got it for me in a few days."

"And did it make you see things—like mystical visions and stuff?"

"No. Not what you could call visions. At first I felt seasick. Not badly. And scared a bit, of course. Like Dr. Jekyll might have felt after he'd taken his drug for the first time. And then certain colors began to get very bright and stand out. You couldn't think why everybody didn't notice them. I remember a woman's red purse lying on a table in a restaurant—it was like a public scandal! And people's faces turn into caricatures; I mean, you seem to see what each

77

one is about, and it's very crude and simplified. One's absurdly vain, and another is literally worrying himself sick, and another is longing to pick a fight. And then you see a very few who are simply beautiful, just cause they aren't anxious or aggressive about anything; they're taking life as it comes. . . . Oh, and everything becomes more and more three-dimensional: Curtains get heavy and sculptured-looking, and wood is very grainy. And flowers and plants are quite obviously alive. I remember a pot of violets—they weren't moving, but you knew they could move. Each one was like a snake reared up motionless on its coils. . . . And then, while the thing is working full strength, it's as if the walls of the room and everything around you are breathing, and the grain in woodwork begins to flow, as though it were a liquid. . . . And then it all slowly dies down again, back to normal. You don't have any hangover. Afterwards I felt fine. I ate a huge supper."

"You didn't take it again after that?"

"No. I found I didn't want to, particularly. It was just an experience I'd had. I gave the rest of the capsules to friends. One of them saw pretty much what I saw, and another didn't see anything. And one told me she'd never been so scared in her whole life. But I suspect she was only being polite. Like thanking for a party—"

"You don't have any of those capsules left now, do you, sir?"

"No, Kenny, I do not! And even if I had, I wouldn't distribute them among the student body. I can think of much more amusing ways to get myself thrown out of this place."

Kenny grins. "Sorry, sir. I was only wondering. . . . I guess, if I really wanted the stuff, I could get it all right. You can get most anything of that kind, right here on campus. This friend of Lois's got it here. *He* claims, when he took it, he saw God."

"Well, maybe he did. Maybe I just didn't take enough."

Kenny looks down at George. He seems amused. "You know something, sir? I bet, even if you *had* seen God, you wouldn't tell us."

"What makes you say that?"

"It's what Lois says. She thinks you're—well, kind of cagey. Like this morning, when you were listening to all that crap we were talking about Huxley—"

"I didn't notice *you* doing much talking. I don't think you opened your mouth once."

"I was watching you. No kidding, I think Lois is right! You let us ramble on, and then you straighten us out, and I'm not saying you don't teach us a lot of interesting stuff—you do—but you never tell us *all* you know about something. . . ."

George feels flattered and excited. Kenny has never talked to him like this before. He can't resist slipping into the role Kenny so temptingly offers him.

"Well—maybe that's true, up to a point. You see, Kenny, there are some things you don't even *know* you know, until you're asked."

They have reached the tennis courts. The courts are all in use now, dotted with moving figures. But

George, with the lizard-quick glance of a veteran addict, has already noted that the morning's pair has left, and that none of these players are physically attractive. On the nearest court, a fat, middle-aged faculty member is playing to work up a sweat, against a girl with hair on her legs.

"Someone has to ask you a question," George continues meaningly, "before you can answer it. But it's so seldom you find anyone who'll ask the right questions. Most people aren't that much interested. . . ."

Kenny is silent. Is he thinking this over? Is he going to ask George something right now? George's pulse quickens with anticipation.

"It's not that I *want* to be cagey," he says, keeping his eyes on the ground and making this as impersonal as he can. "You know, Kenny, so often I feel I want to *tell* things, *discuss* things, absolutely frankly. I don't mean in class, of course—that wouldn't work. Someone would be sure to misunderstand. . . ."

Silence. George glances quickly up at Kenny and sees that he's looking, though without any apparent interest, at the hirsute girl. Perhaps he hasn't even been listening. It's impossible to tell.

"Maybe this friend of Lois's didn't see God, after all," says Kenny abruptly. "I mean, he might have been kidding himself. I mean, not too long after he took the stuff, he had a breakdown. He was locked up for three months in an institution. He told Lois that while he was having this breakdown he turned into a devil and he could put out stars. I'm not kidding! He said he could put out seven of them at a time. He was

80

scared of the police, though. He said the police had a machine for catching devils and liquidating them. It was called a *Mo*-machine. *Mo,* that's *Om*—you know, sir, that Indian word for God—spelled backwards."

"If the police liquidated devils, that would mean they were angels, wouldn't it? Well, that certainly makes sense. A place where the police are angels has to be an insane asylum."

Kenny is still laughing loudly at this when they reach the bookshop. He wants to buy a pencil sharpener. They have them in plastic covers, red or green or blue or yellow. Kenny takes a red one.

"What was it you wanted to get, sir?"

"Well, nothing, actually."

"You mean, you walked all the way down here just to keep me company?"

"Sure. Why not?"

Kenny seems sincerely surprised and pleased. "Well, I think you deserve something for that! Here, sir, take one of these. It's on me."

"Oh, but—well, thank you!" George is actually blushing a little. It's as if he has been offered a rose. He chooses a yellow sharpener.

Kenny grins. "I kind of expected you'd pick blue."

"Why?"

"Isn't blue supposed to be spiritual?"

"What makes you think I want to be spiritual? And how come you picked red?"

"What's red stand for?"

"Rage and lust."

"No kidding?"

81

They remain silent, grinning almost intimately. George feels that, even if all this doubletalk hasn't brought them any closer to understanding each other, the not-understanding, the readiness to remain at cross-purposes, is in itself a kind of intimacy. Then Kenny pays for the pencil sharpeners and waves his hand with a gesture which implies casual, undeferential dismissal. "I'll see you around."

He strolls away. George lingers on in the bookshop for a few minutes, lest he should seem to be following him.

If eating is regarded as a sacrament, then the faculty dining room must be compared to the bleakest and barest of Quaker meetinghouses. No concession here to the ritualism of food served snugly and appetizingly in togetherness. This room is an antirestaurant. It is much too clean, with its chromium-and-plastic tables; much too tidy, with its brown metal wastebaskets for soiled paper napkins and used paper cups; and, in contrast to the vast human rattle of the students' dining room, much too quiet. Its quietness is listless, embarrassed, self-conscious. And the room isn't even made venerable or at least formidable, like an Oxford or Cambridge high table, by the age of its occupants. Most of these people are relatively young; George is one of the eldest.

Christ, it is sad, sad to see on quite a few of these faces—young ones particularly—a glum, defeated look. Why do they feel this way about their lives? Sure, they are underpaid. Sure, they have no great prospects, in the commercial sense. Sure, they can't enjoy the bliss of mingling with corporation executives. But isn't it any consolation to be with students who are still three-quarters alive? Isn't it some tiny satisfaction to be *of use*, instead of helping to turn out useless consumer goods? Isn't it something to know that you belong to one of the few professions in this country which isn't hopelessly corrupt?

For these glum ones, apparently not. They would like out, if they dared try. But they have prepared themselves for this job, and now they have got to go through with it. They have wasted the time in which they should have been learning to cheat and grab and lie. They have cut themselves off from the majority— the middlemen, the hucksters, the promoters—by laboriously acquiring all this dry, discredited knowledge—discredited, that is to say, by the middleman, because he can get along without it. All the middleman wants are its products, its practical applications. These professors are suckers, he says. What's the use of knowing something if you don't make money out of it? And the glum ones more than half agree with him and feel privately ashamed of not being smart and crooked.

83

George goes through into the serving room. On the counter are steaming casseroles from which the waitresses dish you out stew, vegetables or soup. Or you can have salad or fruit pie or a strange deadly-looking jelly which is semitransparent, with veins of brilliant green. Gazing at one of these jellies with a kind of unwilling fascination, as though it were something behind glass in a reptile house, is Grant Lefanu, the young physics professor who writes poetry. Grant is the very opposite of glum, and he couldn't be less defeated; George rather loves him. He is small and thin, and has glasses and large teeth and the maddish smile of genuine intellectual passion. You can easily imagine him as one of the terrorists back in Czarist Russia a hundred years ago. Given the opportunity, he would be that kind of fanatic hero who follows an idea, without the least hesitation and as a matter of course, straight through to its expression in action. The talk of pale, burning-eyed students, anarchists and utopians all, over tea and cigarettes in a locked room long past midnight, is next morning translated, with the literalness of utter innocence, into the throwing of the bomb, the shouting of the proud slogan, the dragging away of the young dreamer-doer, still smiling, to the dungeon and the firing squad. On Grant's face you often see such a smile—of embarrassment, almost, at having had to express his meaning so crudely. He is like a shy mumbler who suddenly in desperation speaks much too loud.

As a matter of fact, Grant has recently performed at least one act of minor heroism. He has appeared in court as a defense witness for a bookseller caught peddling some grand old sex classic of the twenties; it used to be obtainable only in the lands of the Latins, but now, through a series of test cases, it is fighting for its right to be devoured by American youth. (George can't be absolutely sure if this is the same book he himself read as a young man, during a trip to Paris. At all events, he remembers throwing this, or some other book just like it, into the wastebasket, in the middle of the big screwing scene. Not that one isn't broad-minded, of course; let them write about heterosexuality if they must, and let everyone read it who cares to. Just the same, it is a deadly bore and, to be frank, a wee bit distasteful. Why can't these modern writers stick to the old simple wholesome themes—such as, for example, boys?)

Grant Lefanu's heroism on this occasion consisted in his defense of the book at the risk of his academic neck. For a very important and senior member of the STSC faculty had previously appeared as a witness for the prosecution and had guaranteed the book dirty, degenerate and dangerous. When Grant was called to the stand and cross-examined by the prosecuting attorney, he begged, with his shy smile, to differ from his colleague. At length, after some needling and after having been cautioned three times to speak up, he blurted out a statement to the effect that it wasn't the book, but its attackers, who deserved the three adjectives. To make matters worse, one of the local liberal columnists gleefully reported all of this, casting the senior faculty member as a reactionary

85

old ass and Grant as a bright young upholder of civil liberty, and twisting his testimony into a personal insult. So now the question is, Will Grant get his tenure prolonged at the end of the academic year?

Grant treats George as a fellow subverter, a compliment which George hardly deserves, since, with his seniority, his license to play the British eccentric, and, in the last resort, his little private income, he can afford to say pretty much anything he likes on campus. Whereas poor Grant has no private income, a wife and three imprudently begotten children.

"What's new?" George asks him, implying, What has the Enemy been up to?

"You know those courses for police students? Today a special man from Washington is addressing them on twenty ways to spot a Commie."

"You're kidding!"

"Want to go? We might ask him some awkward questions."

"What time is it?"

"Four-thirty."

"Can't. I've got to be downtown in an hour."

"Too bad."

"Too bad," George agrees, relieved. He isn't absolutely sure if this was a bona fide dare or not, however. Various other times, in the same half-serious tone, Grant has suggested that they go and heckle a John Birch Society meeting, smoke pot in Watts with the best unknown poet in America, meet someone high up in the Black Muslim movement. George doesn't seriously suspect Grant of trying to test him.

No doubt Grant really does do such things now and then, and it simply does not occur to him that George might be scared. He probably thinks George excuses himself from these outings for fear of being bored.

As they move down the counter, ending up with only coffee and salad—George watches his weight and Grant has an appetite as slender as his build—Grant tells about a man he knows who has been talking to some experts at a big firm which makes computers. These experts say that it doesn't really matter if there's a war, because enough people will survive to run the country with. Of course, the people who survive will tend to be those with money and influence, because they'll have the better type of shelter, not the leaky death traps which a lot of crooks have been offering at bargain prices. When you get your shelter built, say the experts, you should go to at least three different contractors, so nobody will know what it is you're building; because if the word gets around that you have a better type shelter, you'll be mobbed at the first emergency. For the same reason, you ought to be realistic and buy a submachine gun. This is no time for false sentiment.

George laughs in an appropriately sardonic manner, since this is what Grant expects of him. But this gallows humor sickens his heart. In all those old crises of the twenties, the thirties, the war—each one of them has left its traces upon George, like an illness—what was terrible was the fear of annihilation. Now we have with us a far more terrible fear, the fear of survival. Survival into a Rubble Age, in which it will be quite natural for Mr. Strunk to gun down Grant and his wife and three children, because Grant has neglected to lay in sufficient stores of food and they are starving and may therefore possibly become dangerous and this is no time for sentiment.

"There's Cynthia," Grant says, as they re-enter the dining room. "Want to join her?"

"Do we have to?"

"I guess so. Grant giggles nervously. "She's seen us."

And, indeed, Cynthia Leach is waving to them. She is a handsome young New Yorker, Sarah Lawrence-trained, the daughter of a rich family. Maybe it was partly to annoy them that she recently married Leach, who teaches history here. But their marriage seems to work quite well. Though Andy is slim and white-skinned, he is no weakling; his dark eyes sparkle sexily and he has the unaggressive litheness of one who takes a great deal of exercise in bed. He is somewhat out of his league socially, but no doubt he enjoys the extra effort required to keep up with Cynthia. They give parties to which everyone comes because the food and drink are lavish, thanks to Cynthia's money, and Andy is popular anyhow, and Cynthia isn't that bad. Her only trouble is that she thinks of herself as an Eastern aristocrat slumming; she tries to be patrician and is merely patronizing.

"Andy stood me up," Cynthia tells them. "Talk to me." Then, as they sit down at her table, she turns to Grant. "Your wife's never going to forgive me."

"Oh?" Grant laughs with quite extraordinary violence.

"She didn't tell you about it?"

"Not a word!"

"She didn't?" Cynthia is disappointed. Then she
brightens. "Oh, but she *must* be mad at me! I was telling her how hideously they dress the children here."

"But she agreed with you, I'm sure. She's always
talking about it."

"They're being cheated out of their childhood,"
Cynthia says, ignoring this, "They're being turned
into *junior consumers!* All those dreadful dainty little
creatures, wearing lipstick! I was down in Mexico
last month. It was like a breath of fresh air. Oh, I
can't tell you! Their children are so real. No anxiety.
No other-direction. They just bloom."

"The only question is—" Grant begins. Obviously
he is starting not to agree with Cynthia. For this very
reason, he mumbles, he can barely be heard. Cynthia
chooses not to hear him.

"And then that night we came back across the border! Shall I ever forget it? I said to myself, Either
these people are insane or I am. They all seemed to
be *running,* the way they do in the old silent news-
reels. And the *hostess* in the restaurant—it had never
struck me before how truly sinister it is to call them
that. The way she *smiled* at us! And those enormous
menus, with nothing on them that was really edible.
And those weird zombie busboys, bringing nothing
but glasses of *water* and simply refusing to speak to

you! I just could not believe my own eyes. Oh, and then we stayed the night at one of these ghastly new motels. I had the feeling that it had only just been brought from someplace else, some factory, and set up exactly one minute before we arrived. It didn't belong *anywhere*. I mean—after all those marvelous old hotels in Mexico—each one of them is really a *place*—but this was just utterly unreal—"

Again, Grant seems about to attempt some kind of a protest. But this time his mumbling is still lower. Even George can't understand him. George takes a big drink of his coffee, feels the kick of it in his nearly empty stomach, and finds himself suddenly high. "Really, Cynthia, my dear!" he hears himself exclaim. "How can you talk such incredible nonsense?"

Grant giggles with astonishment. Cynthia looks surprised but rather pleased. She is the kind of bully who likes being challenged; it soothes the itch of her aggression.

"Honestly! Are you out of your mind?" George feels himself racing down the runway, becoming smoothly, exhilaratingly airborne. "My God, you sound like some dreary French intellectual who's just set foot in New York for the first time! That's exactly the way they talk! *Unreal!* American motels are unreal! My good girl—you know and I know that our motels are deliberately designed to be unreal, if you must use that idiotic jargon, for the very simple reason that an American motel room isn't *a* room in *an* hotel, it's *the* room, definitively, period. There is only one: *The Room*. And it's a symbol—an advertisement in three dimensions, if you like—for our way of life. And what's our way of life? A building code which demands certain measurements, certain utilities and the use of certain apt materials; no more and no less. Everything else you've got to supply for yourself. But just try telling that to the Europeans! It scares them to death. The truth is, our way of life is far too austere for them. We've reduced the things of the material plane to mere symbolic conveniences. And why? Because that's the essential first step. Until the material plane has been defined and relegated to its proper place, the mind can't ever be truly free. One would think that was obvious. The stupidest American seems to understand it intuitively. But the Europeans call us inhuman—or they prefer to say immature, which sounds ruder—because we've renounced their world of individual differences and romantic inefficiency and objects-for-the-sake-of-objects. All that dead old cult of cathedrals and first editions and Paris models and vintage wines. Naturally, they never give up, they keep trying to subvert us, every moment, with their loathsome cult-propaganda. If they ever succeed, we'll be done for. *That's* the kind of subversion the Un-American Activities Committee *ought* to be investigating. The Europeans hate us because we've retired to live inside our advertisments, like hermits going into caves to contemplate. We sleep in symbolic bedrooms, eat symbolic meals, are symbolically entertained—and that terrifies them, that fills them with fury and loathing because they can never understand it. They keep yelling out, 'These people are zombies!' They've got to make themselves believe that, because the alternative is to break down and admit that Americans are able to live like this because, actually, they're a far, far more advanced culture—five hundred, maybe a thousand years ahead of Europe, or anyone else on earth, for that matter. Essentially we're creatures of spirit. Our life is all in the mind. That's why we're completely at home with symbols like the American motel room. Whereas the European has a horror of symbols because he's such a groveling little materialist. . . ."

Some moments before the end of this wild word-flight, George has seen, as it were from a great altitude, Andy Leach enter the dining room. Which is indeed a lucky deliverance, for already George has felt his engines cut out, felt himself losing thrust. So now, with the skill of a veteran pilot, he swoops down to a perfect landing. And the beauty of it is, he appears to stop talking out of mere politeness, because Andy has reached their table.

"Did I miss something?" Andy asks, grinning.

A performer at the circus has no theater curtain to come down and hide him and thus preserve the magic spell of his act unbroken. Poised high on the trapeze under the blazing arcs, he has flashed and pulsed like a star indeed. But now, grounded, unsparkling, unfollowed by spotlights, yet plainly visible to anyone who cares to look at him—they are all watching the clowns—he hurries past the tiers of seats toward the exit. Nobody applauds him any more. Very few spare him a single glance.

Together with this anonymity, George feels a fatigue come over him which is not disagreeable. The tide of his vitality is ebbing fast, and he ebbs with it, content. This is a way of resting. All of a sudden he is much, much older. On his way out to the parking lot he walks differently, with less elasticity, moving his arms and his shoulders stiffly. He slows down. Now and then his steps actually shuffle. His head is bowed. His mouth loosens and the muscles of his cheeks sag. His face takes on a dull dreamy placid look. He hums queerly to himself, with a sound like bees around a hive. From time to time, as he walks, he emits quite loud, prolonged farts.

The hospital stands tall on a sleepy bypassed hill, rising from steep lawns and flowering bushes, within sight of the freeway itself. A tall reminder to the passing motorists—*this is the end of the road, folks*—it has a pleasant aspect, nevertheless. It stands open to all the breezes, and there must be many of its windows from which you can see the ocean and the Palos Verdes headland and even Catalina Island, in the clear winter weather.

The nurses at the reception desk are pleasant, too. They don't fuss you with a lot of questions. If you know the number of the room you want to visit, you don't even have to ask for their permission; you can go right up.

George works the elevator himself. At the second floor it is stopped, and a colored male nurse wheels in a prone patient. She is for surgery, he tells George, so they must descend again to the ground floor where the operating rooms are. George offers respectfully to get off the elevator but the young nurse (who has very sexy muscular arms) says, "You don't have to"; so there he stands, like a spectator at the funeral of a stranger, furtively peeking at the patient. She appears to be fully conscious, but it would be a kind of sacrilege to speak to her, for already she is the dedicated, the ritually prepared victim. She seems to know this and consent to it; to be entirely relaxed in her consent. Her gray hair looks so pretty; it must have been recently waved.

This is the gate, George says to himself.

Must I pass through here, too?

Ah, how the poor body recoils with its every nerve from the sight, the smell, the feel of this place!

Blindly it shies, rears, struggles to escape. That it should ever be brought here—stupefied by their drugs, pricked by their needles, cut by their little knives—what an unthinkable outrage to the flesh! Even if they were to cure it and release it, it could never forget, never forgive. Nothing would be the same any more. It would have lost all faith in itself.

Jim used to moan and complain and raise hell over a head cold, a cut finger, a pile. But Jim was lucky at the end—the only time when luck really counts. The truck hit his car just right; he never felt it. And they never got him into a place like this one. His smashed leavings were of no use to them for their rituals.

Doris' room is on the top floor. The hallway is deserted, for the moment, and the door stands open with a screen hiding the bed. George peeps over the top of the screen before going in. Doris is lying with her face toward the window.

George has gotten quite accustomed by now to the way she looks. It isn't even horrible to him any more, because he has lost his sense of a transformation. Doris no longer seems changed. She is a different creature altogether—this yellow shriveled mannequin with its sticks of arms and legs, withered flesh and hollow belly, making angular outlines under the sheet. What has it to do with that big arrogant animal of a girl? With that body which sprawled stark naked, gaping wide in shameless demand, underneath Jim's naked body? Gross insucking vulva, sly ruthless greedy flesh, in all the bloom and gloss and arrogant

95

resilience of youth, demanding that George shall step aside, bow down and yield to the female prerogative, hide his unnatural head in shame. I am Doris. I am Woman. I am Bitch-Mother Nature. The Church and the Law and the State exist to support me. I claim my biological rights. I demand Jim.

George has sometimes asked himself, Would I ever, even in those days, have wished this on her?

The answer is No. Not because George would be incapable of such fiendishness; but because Doris, then, was infinitely more than Doris, was Woman the Enemy, claiming Jim for herself. No use destroying Doris, or ten thousand Dorises, as long as Woman triumphs. Woman could only be fought by yielding, by letting Jim go away with her on that trip to Mexico. By urging him to satisfy all his curiosity and flattered vanity and lust (vanity, mostly) on the gamble that he would return (as he did) saying, *She's disgusting,* saying, *Never again.*

And wouldn't you be twice as disgusted, Jim, if you could see her now? Wouldn't you feel a crawling horror to think that maybe, even then, her body you fondled and kissed hungrily and entered with your aroused flesh already held seeds of this rottenness? You used to bathe the sores on cats so gently and you never minded the stink of old diseased dogs; yet you had a horror, in spite of yourself, of human sickness and people who were crippled. I know something, Jim. I feel certain of it. You'd refuse absolutely to visit her here. You wouldn't be able to force yourself to do it.

George walks around the screen and into the room, making just the necessary amount of noise. Doris turns her head and sees him, seemingly without surprise. Probably, for her, the line between reality and hallucination is getting very thin. Figures keep appearing, disappearing. If one of them sticks you with a needle, then you can be sure it actually *is* a nurse. George may be George or, again, he may not. For convenience she will treat him as George. Why not? What does it matter either way?

"Hello," she says. Her eyes are a wild brilliant blue in her sick yellow face.

"Hello, Doris."

A good while since, George has stopped bringing her flowers or other gifts. There is nothing of any significance he can bring into this room from the outside now; not even himself. Everything that matters to her is now right here in this room, where she is absorbed in the business of dying. Her preoccupation doesn't seem egotistic, however; it does not exclude George or anyone else who cares to share in it. This preoccupation is with death, and we can all share in that, at any time, at any age, well or ill.

George sits down beside her now and takes her hand. If he had done this even two months ago, it would have been loathsomely false. (One of his most bitterly shameful memories is of a time he kissed her cheek—Was it aggression, masochism? Oh, damn all such words!—right after he found out she'd been to bed with Jim. Jim was there when it happened. When George moved toward her to kiss her, Jim's eyes looked startled and scared, as if he feared George was about to bite her like a snake.) But now taking Doris' hand isn't false, isn't even an act of compassion. It is necessary—he has discovered this on previous visits—in order to establish even partial contact. And holding her hand he feels less embarrassed by her sickness; for the gesture means, *We are on the same road, I shall follow you soon.* He is thus excused from having to ask those ghastly sickroom questions, How are you, how's it going, how do you feel?

Doris smiles faintly. Is it because she's pleased that he has come?

No. She is smiling with amusement, it seems. Speaking low but very distinctly, she says, "I made such a noise, yesterday."

George smiles too, waiting for the joke.

"Was it yesterday?" This is in the same tone, but addressed to herself. Her eyes no longer see him; they look bewildered and a bit scared. Time must have become a very odd kind of mirror-maze for her now; and mazes can change at any instant from being funny to being frightening.

But now the eyes are aware of him again; the bewilderment has passed. "I was screaming. They heard me clear down the hall. They had to fetch the doctor." Doris smiles. This, apparently, is the joke.

"Was it your back?" George asks. The effort to keep sympathy out of his voice makes him speak primly, like someone who is trying to suppress an ungentlemanly native accent. But Doris disregards the question. She is off in some new direction of her own, frowning a little. She asks abruptly, "What time is it?"

"Nearly three."

There is a long silence. George feels a terrible need to say something, anything.

"I was out on the pier the other day. I hadn't been there in ages. And, do you know, they've torn down the old roller-skating rink? Isn't that a shame? It seems as if they can't bear to leave anything the way it used to be. Do you remember that booth where the woman used to read your character from your handwriting? That's gone too—"

He stops short, dismayed.

Can memory really get away with such a crude trick? Seemingly it can. For he has picked the pier from it as casually as you pick a card at random from a magician's deck—and behold, the card has been forced! It was while George and Jim were roller-skating that they first met Doris. (She was with a boy named Norman whom she quickly ditched.) And later they all went to have their handwriting read. And the woman told Jim that he had latent musical talent, and Doris that she had a great capacity for bringing out the best in other people—

Does she remember? Of course she must! George glances at her anxiously. She lies staring at the ceiling, frowning harder.

"What did you say the time was?"

"Nearly three. Four minutes of."

"Look outside in the hall, will you? See if anyone's there."

He gets up, goes to the door, looks out. But before he has even reached it, she has asked with harsh impatience, "Well?"

"There's no one."

"Where's that fucking nurse?" It comes out of her so harshly, so nakedly desperate.

"Shall I go look for her?"

"She knows I get a shot at three. The doctor told her. She doesn't give a shit."

"I'll find her."

"That bitch won't come till she's good and ready."

"I'm sure I can find her."

"No! Stay here."

"Okay."

"Sit down again."

"Sure." He sits down. He knows she wants his hand. He gives it to her. She grips it with astonishing strength.

"George—"

"Yes?"

"You'll stay here till she comes?"

"Of course I will."

Her grip tightens. There is no affection in it, no communication. She isn't gripping a fellow creature. His hand is just something to grip. He dare not ask her about the pain. He is afraid of releasing some obscene horror, something visible and tangible and stinking, right here between them in the room.

Yet he is curious, too. Last time, the nurse told him that Doris has been seeing a priest. (She was raised a Catholic.) And, sure enough, here on the table beside the bed is a little paper book, gaudy and cute as a Christmas card: The Stations of the Cross. . . . Ah, but when the road narrows to the width of this bed, when there is nothing in front of you that is known, dare you disdain any guide? Perhaps Doris has learned something already about the journey ahead of her. But, even supposing that she has and that George could bring himself to ask her, she could never tell him what she knows. For that could only be expressed in the language of the place to which she is going. And that language—though some of us gabble it so glibly—has no real meaning in our world. In our mouths, it is just a lot of words.

Here's the nurse, smiling, in the doorway. "I'm punctual today, you see!" She has a tray with the hypodermic and the ampoules.

"I'll be going," George says, rising at once.

"Oh, you don't have to do that," says the nurse. "If you'll just step outside for a moment. This won't take any time at all."

"I have to go anyway," George says, feeling guilty as one always does about leaving any sickroom. Not that Doris herself makes him feel guilty. She seems to have lost all interest in him. Her eyes are fixed on the needle in the nurse's hand.

"She's been a bad girl," the nurse says. "We can't get her to eat her lunch, can we?"

"Well, so long, Doris. See you again in a couple of days."

"Goodbye, George." Doris doesn't even glance at him, and her tone is utterly indifferent. He is leaving her world and thereby ceasing to exist. He takes her hand and presses it. She doesn't respond. She watches the bright needle as it moves toward her.

Did she *mean* goodbye? This could be, soon will be. As George leaves the room, he looks at her once again over the top of the screen, trying to catch and fix some memory in his mind, to be aware of the occasion or at least of its possibility: the last time I saw her alive.

Nothing. It means nothing. He feels nothing.

As George pressed Doris' hand just now, he knew something: that the very last traces of the Doris who tried to take Jim from him have vanished from this shriveled mannequin, and, with them, the last of his hate. As long as one tiny precious drop of hate remained, George could still find something left in her of Jim. For he hated Jim too, nearly as much as her, while they were away together in Mexico. That has been the bond between him and Doris. And now it is broken. And one more bit of Jim is lost to him forever.

As George drives down the boulevard, the big unwieldy Christmas decorations—reindeer

and jingle bells slung across the street on cables se-
cured to metal Christmas trees—are swinging in a
chill wind. But they are merely advertisments for
Christmas, paid for by the local merchants. Shoppers
crowd the stores and the sidewalks, their faces somewhat bewildered, their eyes reflecting, like polished
buttons, the cynical sparkle of the Yuletide. Hardly
more than a month ago, before Khrushchev agreed to
pull his rockets out of Cuba, they were cramming
the markets, buying the shelves bare of beans, rice
and other foodstuffs, utterly useless, most of them,
for air-raid-shelter cookery, because they can't be
prepared without pints of water. Well, the shoppers
were spared—this time. Do they rejoice? They are too
dull for that, poor dears; they never knew what didn't
hit them. No doubt because of that panic buying,
they have less money now for gifts. But they have
enough. It will be quite a good Christmas, the merchants predict. Everyone can afford to spend at least
something, except, maybe, some of the young hus-
tlers (recognizable at once to experienced eyes like
George's) who stand scowling on the street corners
or staring into shops with the maximum of peripheral
vision.

George is very far, right now, from sneering at any
of these fellow creatures. They may be crude and
mercenary and dull and low, but he is proud, is glad,
is almost indecently gleeful to be able to stand up
and be counted in their ranks—the ranks of that marvelous minority, The Living. They don't know their
luck, these people on the sidewalk, but George knows

103

his—for a little while at least—because he is freshly returned from the icy presence of The Majority, which Doris is about to join.

I am alive, he says to himself, *I am alive!* And life-energy surges hotly through him, and delight, and appetite. How good to be in a body—even this old beat-up carcass—that still has warm blood and live semen and rich marrow and wholesome flesh! The scowling youths on the corners see him as a dodderer, no doubt, or at best as a potential score. Yet he still claims a distant kinship with the strength of their young arms and shoulders and loins. For a few bucks he could get any one of them to climb into the car, ride back with him to his house, strip off butch leather jacket, skin-tight levis, shirt and cowboy boots and take part, a naked, sullen young athlete, in the wrestling bout of his pleasure. But George doesn't want the bought unwilling bodies of these boys. He wants to rejoice in his own body—the tough triumphant old body of a survivor. The body that has outlived Jim and is going to outlive Doris.

He decides to stop by the gym—although this isn't one of his regular days—on his way home.

In the locker room, George takes off his clothes, gets into his sweatsocks, jockstrap and shorts. Shall he put on a tee shirt? He looks at himself in the long mirror. Not too bad. The bulges of flesh over the belt of the shorts are not so noticeable today. The legs are quite good. The chest muscles, when properly flexed, don't sag. And, as long as he doesn't have his spectacles on, he can't see the little wrinkles inside the elbows, above the kneecaps and around the hollow of the sucked-in belly. The neck is loose and scraggy under all circumstances, in all lights, and would look gruesome even if he were half-blind. He has abandoned the neck altogether, like an untenable military position.

Yet he looks—and doesn't he know it!—better than nearly all of his age-mates at this gym. Not because they're in such bad shape—they are healthy enough specimens. What's wrong with them is their fatalistic acceptance of middle age, their ignoble resignation to grandfatherhood, impending retirement and golf. George is different from them because, in some sense which can't quite be defined but which is immediately apparent when you see him naked, *he hasn't given up*. He is still a contender, and they aren't. Maybe it's nothing more mysterious than vanity which gives him this air of a withered boy? Yes, despite his wrinkles, his slipped flesh, his graying hair, his grim-lipped, strutting spryness, you catch occasional glimpses of a ghostly someone else, soft-faced, boyish, pretty. The combination is bizarre, it is older than middle age itself, but it is there.

Looking grimly into the mirror, with distaste and humor, George says to himself, You old ass, who are you trying to seduce? And he puts on his tee shirt.

In the gym there are only three people. It's still too early for the office workers. A big heavy man named Buck—all that remains at fifty of a football player— is talking to a curly-haired young man named Rick, who aspires to television. Buck is nearly nude; his rolling belly bulges indecently over a kind of bikini, pushing it clear down to the bush line. He seems quite without shame. Whereas Rick, who has a very well-made muscular body, wears a gray wool sweatshirt and pants, covering all of it from the neck to the wrists and ankles. "Hi, George" they both say, nodding casually at him; and this, George feels, is the most genuinely friendly greeting he has received all day.

Buck knows all about the history of sport; he is an encyclopedia of batting averages, handicaps, records and scores. He is in the midst of telling how someone took someone else in the seventh round. He mimes the knockout: *"Pow! Pow!* And, boy, he'd *had* it!"

106

Rick listens, seated astride a bench. There is always an atmosphere of leisureliness in this place. A boy like Rick will take three or four hours to work out, and spend most of the time just yakking about show biz, about sport cars, about football and boxing—very seldom, oddly enough, about sex. Perhaps this is partly out of consideration for the morals of the various young kids and early teen-agers who are usually around. When Rick talks to grownups, he is apt to be smart-alecky or actor-sincere; but with the kids he is as unaffected as a village idiot. He clowns for them and does magic tricks and tells them stories, deadpan, about a store in Long Beach (he gives its exact address) where once in a great while, suddenly and without any previous announcement, they declare a Bargain Day. On such days, every customer who spends more than a dollar gets a Jag or a Porsche or an MG for free. (The rest of the time, the place is an ordinary antique shop.) When Rick is challenged to show the car *he* got, he takes the kids outside and points to a suitable one on the street. When they look at its registration slip and find that it belongs to someone else, Rick swears that that's his real name; he changed it when he started acting. The kids don't absolutely disbelieve him, but they yell that he's a liar and crazy and they beat on him with their fists. While they do this, Rick capers grinning around the gym on all fours, like a dog.

George lies down on one of the inclined boards in order to do sit-ups. This is always something you have to think yourself into; the body dislikes them more than any other exercise. While he is getting into the mood, Webster comes over and lies down on the board next to his. Webster is maybe twelve or thirteen, slender and graceful and tall for his age, with long smooth golden boy-legs. He is gentle and shy, and he moves about the gym in a kind of dream; but he keeps steadily on with his workout. No doubt he thinks he looks scrawny and has vowed to become a huge wide awkward overloaded muscle man. George says, "Hi, Web," and Webster answers, "Hi, George," in a shy, secretive whisper.

Now Webster begins doing his sit-ups, and George, peeling off his tee shirt on a sudden impulse, follows his example. As they continue, George feels an empathy growing between them. They are not competing with each other; but Webster's youth and litheness seem to possess George, and this borrowed energy is terrific. Withdrawing his attention from his own protesting muscles and concentrating it upon Webster's flexing and relaxing body, George draws the strength from it to go on beyond his normal forty sit-ups, to fifty, to sixty, to seventy, to eighty. Shall he try for a hundred? Then, all at once, he is aware that Webster has stopped. The strength leaves him instantly. He stops too, panting hard—though not any harder than Webster himself. They lie there panting, side by side. Webster turns his head and looks at George, obviously rather impressed.

"How many do you do?" he asks.

"Oh—it depends."

"These things just kill me. Man!"

108

How delightful it is to be here. If only one could spend one's entire life in this state of easygoing physical democracy. Nobody is bitchy here, or ill-tempered, or inquisitive. Vanity, including the most outrageous posings in front of the mirrors, is taken for granted. The godlike young baseball player confides to all his anxiety about the smallness of his ankles. The plump banker, rubbing his face with skin cream, says simply, "I can't afford to get old." No one is perfect and no one pretends to be. Even the half-dozen quite well-known actors put on no airs. The youngest kids sit innocently naked beside sixty- and seventy-year-olds in the steam room, and they call each other by their first names. Nobody is too hideous or too handsome to be accepted as an equal. Surely everyone is nicer in this place than he is outside it?

Today George feels more than usually unwilling to leave the gym. He does his exercises twice as many times as he is supposed to; he spends a long while in the steam room; he washes his hair.

When he comes out onto the street again, it is already getting toward sunset. And now he makes another impulsive decision: instead of driving directly back to the beach, he will take a long detour through the hills.

Why? Partly because he wants to enjoy the uncomplicated relaxed happy mood which is nearly always produced by a workout at the gym. It is so good to feel the body's satisfaction and gratitude; no matter how much it may protest, it likes being forced to perform these tasks. Now, for a while at least, the vagus nerve won't twitch, the pylorus will be quiet, the arthritic thumbs and knee won't assert themselves. And how restful, now that there's no need for stimulants, not to have to hate anyone at all! George hopes to be able to stay in this mood as long as he keeps on driving.

Also, he wants to take a look at the hills again; he hasn't been up there in a long time. Years ago, before Jim even, when George first came to California, he used to go into the hills often. It was the wildness of this range, largely uninhabited yet rising right up out of the city, that fascinated him. He felt the thrill of being a foreigner, a trespasser there, of venturing into the midst of a primitive, alien nature. He would drive up at sunset or very early in the morning, park his car, and wander off along the firebreak trails, catching glimpses of deer moving deep in the chaparral of a canyon, stopping to watch a hawk circling overhead, stepping carefully among hairy tarantulas crawling across his path, following twisty tracks in the sand until he came upon a coiled dozing rattler. Sometimes, in the half-light of dawn, he would meet a pack of coyotes trotting toward him, tails down, in single file. The first time this happened he took them for dogs; and then, suddenly, without uttering a sound, they broke formation and went bounding away downhill, with great uncanny jumps.

But this afternoon George can feel nothing of that long-ago excitement and awe; something is wrong from the start. The steep, winding road, which used to seem romantic, is merely awkward now, and dangerous. He keeps meeting other cars on blind corners and having to swerve sharply. By the time he has reached the top, he has lost all sense of relaxation. Even up here they are building dozens of new houses. The area is getting suburban. True, there are still a few uninhabited canyons, but George can't rejoice in them; he is oppressed by awareness of the city below. On both sides of the hills, to the north and to the south, it has spawned and spread itself over the entire plain. It has eaten up the wide pastures and ranchlands and the last stretches of orange grove; it has sucked out the surrounding lakes and sapped the forests of the high mountains. Soon it will be drinking converted sea water. And yet it will die. No need for rockets to wreck it, or another ice age to freeze it, or a huge earthquake to crack it off and dump it in the Pacific. It will die of overextension. It will die because its taproots have dried up—the brashness and greed which have been its only strength. And the desert, which is the natural condition of this country, will return.

Alas, how sadly, how certainly George knows this!

111

He stops the car and stands at the road's rough yellow dirt edge, beside a manzanita bush, and looks out over Los Angeles like a sad Jewish prophet of doom, as he takes a leak. *Babylon is fallen, is fallen, that great city.* But this city is not great, was never great, and has nearly no distance to fall.

Now he zips up his pants and gets into the car and drives on, thoroughly depressed. The clouds close in low upon the hills, making them seem northern and sad like Wales; and the day wanes, and the lights snap on in their sham jewel colors all over the plain, as the road winds down again on to Sunset Boulevard and he nears the ocean.

The supermarket is still open; it won't close till midnight. It is brilliantly bright. Its brightness offers sanctuary from loneliness and the dark. You could spend hours of your life here, in a state of suspended insecurity, meditating on the multiplicity of things to eat. Oh dear, there is so much! So many brands in shiny boxes, all of them promising you good appetite. Every article on the shelves cries out to you, Take me, take me; and the mere competition

112

of their appeals can make you imagine yourself wanted, even loved. But beware—when you get back to your empty room, you'll find that the false flattering elf of the advertisment has eluded you; what remains is only cardboard, cellophane and food. And you have lost the heart to be hungry.

This bright place isn't really a sanctuary. For, ambushed among its bottles and cartons and cans, are shockingly vivid memories of meals shopped for, cooked, eaten with Jim. They stab out at George as he passes, pushing his shopping cart. Should we ever feel truly lonely if we never ate alone?

But to say, I won't eat alone tonight—isn't that deadly dangerous? Isn't it the start of a long landslide—from eating at counters and drinking at bars to drinking at home without eating, to despair and sleeping pills and the inevitable final overdose? But who says I have to be brave? George asks. Who depends on me now? Who cares?

We're getting maudlin, he says, trying to make his will choose between halibut, sea bass, chopped sirloin, steaks. He feels a nausea of distaste for them all; then sudden rage. Damn all food. Damn all life. He would like to abandon his shopping cart, although it's already full of provisions. But that would make extra work for the clerks, and one of them is cute. The alternative, to put the whole lot back in the proper places himself, seems like a labor of Hercules; for the overpowering sloth of sadness is upon him. The sloth that ends in going to bed and staying there until you develop some disease.

So he wheels the cart to the cash desk, pays, stops on the way out to the car lot, enters the phone booth, dials.

"Hello."

"Hello, Charley."

"*Geo!*"

"Look—is it too late to change my mind? About to-night? You see—when you called this morning—I thought I had this date—But I just heard from them that—"

"*Of course* it isn't too late!" She doesn't even bother to listen to his lying excuses. Her gladness flashes its instantaneous way to him, even faster than her words, across the zigzag of the wires. And at once Geo and Charley are linked, are yet another of this evening's lucky pairs, amidst all of its lonely wanderers. If any of the clerks were watching, they would see his face inside the glass box brighten, flush with joy like a lover's.

"Can I bring you anything? I'm at the market—"

"Oh no—no thank you, Geo dear! I have loads of food. I always seem to get too much nowadays. I suppose it's because . . ."

"I'll be over in a little while then. Have to stop by the house, first. So long."

"Oh, Geo—this *is* nice! Au revoir!"

But he is so utterly perverse that his mood begins to change again before he has even finished unloading his purchases into the car. Do I really want to see her? he asks himself, and then, What in the world made me do that? He pictures the evening he might

114

have spent, snugly at home, fixing the food he has bought, then lying down on the couch beside the bookcase and reading himself slowly sleepy. At first glance this is an absolutely convincing and charming scene of domestic contentment. Only after a few instants does George notice the omission that makes it meaningless. What is left out of the picture is Jim, lying opposite him at the other end of the couch, also reading; the two of them absorbed in their books yet so completely aware of each other's presence.

Back at home, he changes out of his suit into an army-surplus store khaki shirt, faded blue denims, moccasins, a sweater. (He has had doubts from time to time about this kind of costume: Doesn't it give the impression that he's trying to dress young? But Jim used to tell him, No, it was just right for him —it made him look like Rommel in civilian clothes. George loved that.)

Just when he's ready to leave the house again, there is a ring at his doorbell. Who can it be at this hour?

Mrs. Strunk!

(What have I done that she can have come to complain about?)

"Oh, good evening—" (Obviously she's nervous, self-conscious; very much aware, no doubt, of having crossed the frontier-bridge and being on enemy territory.) "I know this is terribly short notice. I—we've meant to ask you so many times—I know how busy you are—but we haven't gotten together in such a long while—and we were wondering—would you possibly have time to come over for a drink?"

"You mean, right now?"

"Why, yes. There's just the two of us at home."

"I'm most terribly sorry. I'm afraid I have to go out, right away."

"Oh. Well. I was afraid you wouldn't have time. But—"

"No, listen," says George, and he means it; he is extremely surprised and pleased and touched. "I really *would* like to. Very much indeed. Do you suppose I could take a rain-check?"

"Well, yes, of course." But Mrs. Strunk doesn't believe him. She smiles sadly. Suddenly it seems all-important to George to convince her.

"I would *love* to come. How about tomorrow?"

Her face falls. "Oh well, tomorrow. Tomorrow wouldn't be so good, I'm afraid. You see, tomorrow we have some friends coming over from the Valley, and . . ."

And they might notice something queer about me, and you'd feel ashamed, George thinks, okay, okay.

116

"I understand, of course," he says. "But let's make it very soon, shall we?"

"Oh *yes*," she agrees fervently, *"very* soon. . . ."

Charlotte lives on Soledad Way, a narrow uphill street which at night is packed so tight with cars parked on both sides of it that two drivers can scarcely squeeze past each other. If you arrive after its residents have returned home from their jobs, you will probably have to leave your car several blocks away, at the bottom of the hill. But this is no problem for George, because he can walk over to Charley's from his house in less than five minutes.

Her house is high up on the hillside, at the top of three flights of lopsided rustic wooden steps, seventy-five of them in all. Down on the street level there is a tumbledown shack intended for a garage. She keeps it crammed to the ceiling with battered trunks and crates full of unwanted junk. Jim used to say that she kept the garage blocked in order not to be able to own a car. In any case, she absolutely refuses to learn to drive. If she needs to go someplace and no one offers to give her a ride, well then, that's too bad, she can't go. But the neighbors nearly always do help her; she has them utterly intimidated and bewitched by this Britishness which George himself knows so well how to employ, though with a different approach.

The house next to Charlotte's is on the street level. As you begin to climb her steps, you get an intimate glimpse of domestic squalor through its bathroom window (it must be frankly admitted that Soledad is one whole degree socially inferior to Camphor Tree Lane): a tub hung with panties and diapers, a douche bag slung over the shower pipe, a plumber's snake on the floor. None of the neighbor's kids are visible now, but you can see how the hillside above their home has been trampled into a brick-hard slippery surface with nothing alive on it but some cactus. At the top of the slope there is a contraption like a gallows, with a net for basketball attached to it.

Charlotte's slice of the hill can still just be described as a garden. It is terraced, and a few of the roses on it are in bloom. But they have been sadly neglected; when Charley is in one of her depressive moods, even the poor plants must suffer for it. They have been allowed to grow out into a tangle of long thorny shoots, with the weeds thick between them.

George climbs slowly, taking it easy. (Only the very young are not ashamed to arrive panting.) These outdoor staircases are a feature of the neighborhood. A few of them have the original signs on their steps which were painted by the bohemian colonists and addressed, apparently, to guests who were clambering upstairs on their hands and knees, drunk: Upward and onward. Never weaken. You're in bad shape, sport. Hey—you can't die *here!* Ain't this *heaven?*

The staircases have become, as it were, the instruments of the colonists' posthumous vengeance on their supplanters, the modern housewives; for they defy all labor-saving devices. Short of bringing in a giant crane, there is absolutely no way of getting anything up them except by hand. The icebox, the stove, the bathtub and all of the furniture have had to be pushed and dragged up to Charley's by strong, savagely cursing men. Who then clapped on huge extra charges and expected triple tips.

Charley comes out of the house as he nears the top. She has been watching for him, as usual, and no doubt fearing some last-moment change in his plans. They meet on the tiny unsafe wooden porch outside the front door, and hug. George feels her soft bulky body pressed against his. Then, abruptly, she releases him with a smart pat on the back, as much as to show him that she isn't going to overdo the affection; she knows when enough is enough.

"Come along in with you," she says.

Before following her indoors, George casts a glance out over the little valley to the line of boardwalk lamps where the beach begins and the dark unseen ocean. This is a mild windless night, with streaks of sea fog dimming the lights in the houses below. From this porch, when the fog is really thick, you can't see the houses at all and the lights are just blurs,

119

and Charlotte's nest seems marvelously remote from everywhere else in the world.

It is a simple rectangular box, one of those prefabs which were put up right after the War. Newspapers enthused over them, they were acclaimed as the homes of the future; but they didn't catch on. The living room is floored with tatami, and more than somewhat Oriental-gift-shop in decor. A teahouse lantern by the door, wind bells at the windows, a huge red paper fish-kite pinned to the wall. Two picture scrolls: a madly Japanese tiger snarling at a swooping (American ?) eagle; an immortal sitting under a tree, with half a dozen twenty-foot hairs growing out of his chin. Three low couches littered with gay silk cushions, too tiny for any useful purpose but perfect for throwing at people.

"I say, I've just realized that there's a most ghastly smell of cooking in here!" Charlotte exclaims. There certainly is. George answers politely that it's a delicious smell and that it makes him hungry.

"I'm trying a new kind of stew, as a matter of fact. I got the idea from a marvelous travel book Myrna Custer just brought me—about Borneo. Only the author gets slightly vague, so I've had to improvise a bit. I mean, he doesn't come right out and say so, but I have a suspicion that one's *supposed* to make it with human flesh. Actually, I've used leftovers from a joint . . ."

She is a lot younger than George—forty-five next birthday—but, already, like him, she is a survivor. She has the survivor's typical battered doggedness.

To judge from photographs, she was adequately pretty as long as her big gray eyes were combined with soft youthful coloring. Her poor cheeks are swollen and inflamed now, and her hair, which must once have made a charming blur around her face, is merely untidy. Nevertheless, she hasn't given up. Her dress shows a grotesque kind of gallantry, ill-advised but endearing: an embroidered peasant blouse in bold colors, red, yellow and violet, with the sleeves rolled up to the elbows; a gipsyish Mexican skirt which looks as if she had girded it on like a blanket, with a silver-studded cowboy belt—it only emphasizes her lack of shape. Oh, and if she must wear sandals with bare feet, why won't she make up her toenails? (Maybe a lingering middle-class Midlands puritanism is in operation here.) Jim once said to her kiddingly about a similar outfit, "I see you've adopted our native costume, Charley." She laughed, not at all offended, but she didn't get the point. She hasn't gotten it yet. This *is* her idea of informal Californian playwear, and she honestly cannot see that she dresses any differently from Mrs. Peabody next door.

"Have I told you, Geo? No, I'm sure I haven't. I've already made two New Year's resolutions—only they're effective immediately. The first is, I'm going to admit that I loathe bourbon." (She pronounces it like the dynasty, not the drink.) "I've been pretending not to, ever since I came to this country—all because Buddy drank it. But, let's face it, who do I think I'm kidding *now?*" She smiles at George very bravely and brightly, reassuring him that this is *not*

121

a prelude to an attack of the Buddy-blues; then quickly continues, "My other resolution is that I'm going to stop denying that that infuriating accusation is true: Women *do* mix drinks too strong, damn it! I suppose it's part of our terrible anxiety to please. So let's begin the new regime as of now, shall we? You come and mix your own drink and mine too— and I'd like a vodka and tonic, please."

She has obviously had at least a couple already. Her hands fumble as she lights a cigarette. (The Indonesian ashtray is full, as usual, of lipstick-marked stubs.) Then she leads the way into the kitchen with her curious rolling gait which is nearly a limp, suggesting arthritis and the kind of toughness that goes with it.

"It *was* sweet of you to come tonight, Geo."

He grins suitably, says nothing.

"You broke your other appointment, didn't you?"

"I did not! I told you on the phone—these people canceled at the last minute—"

"Oh, Geo dear, come off it! You know, I sometimes think, about you, whenever you do something really sweet, you're ashamed of it afterwards! You knew jolly well how badly I needed you tonight, so you broke that appointment. I could tell you were fibbing, the minute you opened your mouth! You and I can't pull the wool over each other's eyes. *I* found that out, long ago. Haven't *you*—after all these years?"

"I certainly should have," he agrees, smiling and thinking what an absurd and universally accepted bit of nonsense it is that your best friends must necessarily be the ones who best understand you. As if there weren't far too much understanding in the world already; above all, that understanding between lovers, celebrated in song and story, which is actually such torture that no two of them can bear it without frequent separations or fights. Dear old Charley, he thinks, as he fixes their snorts in her cluttered, none-too-clean kitchen, how could I have gotten through these last years without your wonderful lack of perception? How many times, when Jim and I had been quarreling and came to visit you—sulking, avoiding each other's eyes, talking to each other only through you—did you somehow bring us together again by the sheer power of your unawareness that anything was wrong?

And now, as George pours the vodka (giving her a light one, to slow her down) and the Scotch (giving himself a heavier one, to catch up on), he begins to feel this utterly mysterious unsensational thing—not bliss, not ecstasy, not joy—just plain happiness. *Das Glueck, le bonheur, la felicidad*—they have given it all three genders, but one has to admit, however grudgingly, that the Spanish are right; it is usually feminine, that's to say, woman-created. Charley creates it astonishingly often; this doubtless is something else she isn't aware of, since she can do it even when she herself is miserable. As for George, his felicidad is sublimely selfish; he can enjoy it unperturbed while Charley is in the midst of Buddy-blues or a Fred-crisis (one is brewing this evening, obviously).

123

However, there are unlucky occasions when you get her blues without your felicidad, and it's a graveyard bore. But not this evening. This evening he is going to enjoy himself.

Charlotte, meanwhile, has peeked into the oven and then closed its door again, announcing, "Twenty more minutes" with the absolute confidence of a great chef, which by God she isn't.

As they walk back into the living room with their drinks, she tells him, "Fred called me—late last night." This is said in her flat, underplayed crisis-tone.

"Oh?" George manages to sound sufficiently surprised. "Where is he now?"

"Palo Alto." Charlotte sits down on the couch under the paper fish, with conscious drama, as though she has said, "Siberia."

"Palo Alto—he was there before, wasn't he?"

"Of course he was. That's where that girl lives. He's with her, naturally. . . . I *must* learn not to say 'that girl.' She's got a perfectly good name, and I can hardly pretend I don't know it: Loretta Marcus. Anyhow, it's none of my business who Fred's with or what she does with Fred. Her mother doesn't seem to care. Well, never mind any of that. . . . We had a long talk. This time, he really was quite sweet and reasonable about the whole situation. At least, I could feel how hard he was trying to be . . . Geo, it's no good our going on like this. He *has* made up his mind, really and truly. He wants a complete break."

Her voice is trembling ominously. George says

124

without conviction, "He's awfully young, still."

"He's awfully old for his age. Even two years ago he could have looked after himself if he'd had to. Just because he's a minor, I can't treat him like a child—I mean, and use the law to make him come back. Besides, then, he'd *never* forgive me—"

"He's changed his mind before this."

"Oh, I know. And I know you think he hasn't behaved well to me, Geo. I don't blame you for thinking that. I mean, it's natural for you to take my side. And then, you've never had any children of your own. You don't mind my saying that, Geo dear? Oh, I'm sorry—"

"Don't be silly, Charley."

"Even if you had had children, it wouldn't really be the same. This mother and son thing—I mean, especially when you've had to bring him up without a father—that's really hell. I mean, you try and you try—but everything you do or say seems to turn out wrong. I smother him—he said that to me once. At first I couldn't understand—I just couldn't accept it—but now I do—I've got to—and I honestly *think* I do —he must live his own life—right away from me— even if he begs me to, I simply mustn't see him for a long long while—I'm sorry, Geo—I didn't mean to do this—I'm so—sorry—"

George moves closer to her on the couch, puts one arm around her, squeezes her sobbing plumpness gently, without speaking. He is not cold; he is not unmoved. He is truly sorry for Charley and this mess —and yet—la felicidad remains intact; he is very much at his ease. With his free hand, he helps himself to a sip of his drink, being careful not to let the movement be felt through the engaged side of his body.

But how very strange to sit here with Charley sobbing and remember that night when the long-distance call came through from Ohio. An uncle of Jim's whom he'd never met—trying to be sympathetic, even admitting George's right to a small honorary share in the sacred family grief—but then, as they talked, becoming a bit chilled by George's laconic *Yes, I see, yes,* his curt *No, thank you,* to the funeral invitation—deciding no doubt that this much talked of roommate hadn't been such a close friend, after all. . . . And then, at least five minutes after George had put down the phone, when the first shock wave hit, when the meaningless news suddenly meant exactly what it said, his blundering gasping run up the hill in the dark, his blind stumbling on the steps, banging at Charley's door, crying blubbering howling on her shoulder, in her lap, all over her; and Charley squeezing him, stroking his hair, telling him the usual stuff one tells. . . . Late next afternoon, as he shook himself out of the daze of the sleeping pills she'd given him, he felt only disgust: I betrayed you, Jim; I betrayed our life together; I made you into a sob story for a skirt. But that was just hysteria, part of the second shock wave. It soon passed. And meanwhile Charley, bless her silly heart, took the situation over more and more completely—cooking his meals and bringing them down to the

126

house while he was out, the dishes wrapped in tinfoil ready to be reheated; leaving him notes urging him to call her at any hour he felt the need, the deader of night the better; hiding the truth from her friends with such visibly sealed lips that they must surely have suspected Jim had fled the state after some sex scandal—until at last she had turned Jim's death into something of her own creation entirely, a roaring farce. (George is grinning to himself, now.) Oh yes indeed, he is glad that he ran to her that night. That night, in purest ignorance, she taught him a lesson he will never forget—namely, that you can't betray (that idiotic expression!) a Jim, or a life with a Jim, even if you try to.

By now, Charlotte has sobbed herself into a calm. After a couple of sniffs, she says "sorry" again, and stops.

"I keep wondering just when it began to go wrong."

"Oh, Charley, for Heaven's sake, what good does that do?"

"Of course, if Buddy and I had stayed together—"

"No one can say that was your fault."

"It's always both people's."

"Do you hear from him nowadays?"

"Oh yes, every so often. They're still in Scranton. He's out of a job. And Debbie just had another baby —that's their third—another daughter. I can't think how they manage. I keep trying to stop him sending any more money, even though it is for Fred. But he's so obstinate, poor lamb, when he thinks something's

127

his duty. Well, from now on, I suppose he and Fred will have to work that out between them. I'm out of the picture altogether—"

There is a bleak little pause. George gives her an encouraging pat on the shoulder. "How about a couple of quick ones before that stew?"

"I think that's a positively brilliant idea!" She laughs quite gaily. But then, as he takes the glass from her, she strokes his hand with a momentary return to pathos, "you're so damned good to me, Geo." Her eyes fill with tears. However, he can decently pretend that he hasn't noticed them, so he walks away.

If I'd been the one the truck hit, he says to himself, as he enters the kitchen, Jim would be right here, this very evening, walking through this doorway, carrying these two glasses. Things are as simple as that.

So here we are," Charlotte says, "just the two of us. Just you and me."

They are drinking their coffee after dinner. The stew turned out quite a success, though not noticeably different from all Charlotte's other stews, its relationship to Borneo being almost entirely literary.

"Just the two of us," she repeats.

George smiles at her vaguely, not sure yet if this is a lead-in to something, or only sententious-sentimental warmth arising from the wine. They had about a bottle and a half between them.

But then, slowly, thoughtfully, as though this were a mere bit of irrelevant feminine musing, she adds, "I suppose, in a day or two, I must get around to cleaning out Fred's room."

A pause.

"I mean, until I've done that, I won't feel that everything's really over. You have to do something, to convince yourself. You know what I mean?"

"Yes, Charley. I think so."

"I shall send Fred anything he needs, of course. The rest I can store away. There's heaps of space under the house."

"Are you planning to rent his room?" George asks —because, if she *is* leading up to something, they may as well get to it.

"Oh no, I couldn't possibly do that. Well, not to a stranger, anyhow. One couldn't offer him any real privacy. He'd have to be part of the family—oh dear, I *must* stop using that expression, it's only force of habit. . . . Still, *you* understand, Geo. It would have to be someone I knew most awfully well—"

"I can see that."

"You know, you and I—it's funny—we're really in the same boat now. Our houses are kind of too big for us, and yet they're too small."

"Depending on which way you look at it."

"Yes. . . . Geo darling—if I ask you something— it's not that I'm trying to pry or anything—"

"Go ahead."

"Now that—well, now that some time has gone by —do you still feel that you want to live alone?"

"I never wanted to live alone, Charley."

"Oh, I *know*! Forgive me. I never meant—"

"I know you didn't. That's perfectly all right."

"Of course, I know how you must feel about that house of yours. . . . You've never thought of moving, have you?"

"No—not seriously."

"No—" (This is a bit wistful.) "I suppose you wouldn't. I suppose—as long as you stay there—you feel closer to Jim. Isn't that it?"

"Maybe that's it."

She reaches over and gives his hand a long squeeze of deep understanding. Then, stubbing out her cigarette (brave, now, for both of them), she says brightly, "Would you like to get us some drinks, Geo?"

"The dishes, first."

"Oh, but darling, let's leave them, please! I'll wash them in the morning. I mean, I'd *like* to. It gives me something to do these days. There's so little—"

"No arguments, Charley! If you won't help me, I'll do them alone."

"Oh, *Geo!*"

And now, half an hour later, they're back in the living room again, with fresh drinks in their hands.

"How can you pretend you don't love it?" she is asking him, with a teasing, coquettish reproachfulness. "And you miss it—you wish you were back there—you *know* you do!" This is one of her favorite themes.

"I'm not pretending anything, Charley, for Heaven's sake! You keep ignoring the fact that I *have* been back there, several times; and you haven't. I'm absolutely willing to admit that I like it better every time I do go. In fact, right now I think it's probably the most extraordinary country in the world—because it's such a marvelous mixup. Everything's changed, and yet nothing has. I don't believe I ever told you this—last year, in the middle of the summer, when Jim and I were over there, you remember, we made a trip through the Cotswolds. Well, one morning we were on this little branch-line train, and we stopped at a village which was right out of a Tennyson poem —sleepy meadows all around, and lazy cows, and

131

moaning doves, and immemorial elms, and the Elizabethan manor house showing through the trees. And there, on the platform, were two porters dressed just the same way porters have been dressed since the nineteenth century. Only they were Negroes from Trinidad. And the ticket collector at the gate was Chinese. I nearly died of joy. I mean, it was the one touch that had been lacking, all these years. It finally made the whole place perfect—"

"I'm not sure how I should like that part of it," says Charlotte. Her romanticism has received a jolt, as he knew it would. Indeed, he has told this story to tease her. But she won't be put off. She wants more. She is just in the mood for tipsy day-dreaming. "And then you went up North, didn't you," she prompts him, "to look at the house you were born in?"

"Yes."

"Tell me about it!"

"Oh, Charley—I've told you dozens of times!"

"Tell me again—*please*, Geo!"

She is as persistent as a child; and George can seldom refuse her, especially after he's had a few drinks.

"It used to be a farmhouse, you know. It was built in 1649—the year they beheaded Charles the First—"

"*1649!* Oh, Geo—just *think* of it!"

"There are several other farms in the neighborhood much older than that. Of course, it's had a lot of alterations. The people who live there now—he's a television producer in Manchester—have practically rebuilt the inside of it. Put in a new staircase and an

132

extra bathroom and modernized the kitchen. And the other day they wrote me that they now have central heating."

"How horrible! There ought to be a law against ruining beautiful old houses. This craze for bringing things up to date—I suppose they've caught it from this bloody country."

"Don't be a goose, Charley darling! The place was all but uninhabitable the way it was. It's built of that local stone which seems to suck up every drop of moisture in the air. And there's plenty, in that ghastly climate. Even in summer the walls used to be clammy; and in winter, if you went into a room where the fire hadn't been lighted for a few days, it was cold as death. The cellar actually smelt like a tomb. Mold was always forming on the books, and the wallpaper kept peeling off, and the mounts of the pictures were spotted with damp. . . ."

"Whatever you say about it, darling, you always make it sound so marvelously romantic. Exactly like *Wuthering Heights!*"

"Actually, it's almost suburban nowadays. You walk down a short lane and there you are on the main road, with buses running every twenty minutes into Manchester."

"But didn't you tell me the house is on the edge of the moors?"

"Well, yes—so it is. That's what's so odd about it. It's kind of in two worlds. When you look out from the back—from the room I was born in, as a matter of fact—that view literally hasn't changed since I was a boy. You still see hardly any houses—just the open hills, and the stone walls running over them, and a few little whitewashed dots of farms. And of course the trees around the old farmyard were planted long, long before I was born, to shelter the house—there's a lot of wind up there, on the ridge—great big beech trees—they make a sort of seething sound, like waves —that's one of the earliest sounds I remember. I sometimes wonder if that's why I always have had this thing about wanting to live near the ocean—"

Something is happening to George. To please Charley, he has started to make magic; and now the magic is taking hold of him. He is quite aware of this —but what's the harm? It's fun. It adds a new dimension to being drunk. Just as long as there's no one to hear him but Charley! She is sighing deeply now with sympathy and delight—the delight of an addict when someone else admits he's hooked, too.

"There's a little pub high up on the moors, the very last house in the village—actually it's on the old coaching road over the hills, which hardly anyone uses now. Jim and I used to go there in the evenings. It's called The Farmer's Boy. The bar parlor has one of those low, very heavy-looking ceilings, you know, with warped oak beams; and there's a big open fireplace. And some foxes' masks mounted on the wall. And an engraving of Queen Victoria riding a pony in the Highlands—"

Charlotte is so delighted that she actually claps her hands. "Geo! Oh, I can just see it all!"

134

"One night we were there, they stayed open extra late, because it was Jim's birthday—that is, they shut the outside door and went right on serving drinks. We felt marvelously cozy, and we drank pints and pints of Guinness, far more than we wanted, just because it was illegal. And then there was a 'character' —that was how they all described him—'Oh, he's a character, he is!' named Rex, who was a kind of a rustic beat. He worked as a farm laborer, but only when he absolutely had to. He started talking in a very superior tone to impress us. He told Jim, 'You Yanks are living in a world of fantasy'! But then he got much more friendly, and when we were walking back to the inn where we were staying, absolutely plastered by this time, Rex and I discovered something in common: we both knew Newbolt's *Vitae Lampada* by heart, we'd learnt it at school. So of course we began roaring out, 'Play up, play up, and play the game!' And when we got to the second verse, about the sands of the desert being sodden red, I said, 'The colonel's jammed and the gatling's dead,' and Rex thought that was the joke of the year, and Jim sat right down on the road, and buried his face in his hands and uttered a terrible groan—"

"You mean, he wasn't enjoying himself?"

"Jim not enjoying himself? He was having the ball of his life! For a while I thought I'd never get him out of England again. And, you know, he fell wildly in love with that pub? The rest of the house is very attractive, I must admit. There's an upstairs sitting

135

room which you could really make something out of. And quite a big garden. Jim wanted us to buy it and live there, and run it together."

"What a marvelous idea! Oh, what a shame you couldn't have!"

"Actually, it wouldn't have been utterly impossible. We made some inquiries. I think we could have persuaded them to sell. And no doubt Jim would have picked up pub-running, the way he did everything else. Of course, there'd have been an awful lot of red tape, and permits, and stuff. . . . Oh yes, we talked about it. We even used to say we'd go back this year and look into the whole thing some more—"

"Do you think—I mean, if Jim—would you *really* have bought it and settled down there?"

"Oh, who knows? We were always making plans like that. We hardly ever told other people about them, even you. Maybe that was because we knew in our hearts they were crazy. But then again, we did do some crazy things, didn't we? Well, we'll never know, now. . . . Charlotte, dear, we are both in need of a drink."

He is suddenly aware of Charlotte saying, "I suppose, for a man, it *is* different. . . ."

(*What's* different? Can he have dozed off for a couple of seconds? George shakes himself awake.)

" . . . You know, I used to think that about Buddy? He could have lived anywhere. He could have traveled hundreds of miles across nowhere and then suddenly just pitched his tent and called it somewhere, and it *would* have been somewhere, simply because he said so. After all, I mean, isn't that what the pioneers all did in this country, not so long ago? It must have been in Buddy's blood—though it certainly can't be any longer. Debbie would never put up with that sort of thing. No, Geo, cross my heart, I am honestly not being bitchy! I wouldn't have put up with it either, in the long run. Women are like that—we've simply got to hang on to our roots. We *can* be transplanted, yes—but it has to be done by a man, and when he's done it, he has to stay with us and wither—I mean water—I mean, the new roots wither if they aren't watered. . . ." Her voice has thickened. Now she gives her head an abrupt shake, just as George did a few moments ago. "Am I making any sense at all?"

"Yes, Charley. Aren't you trying to tell me you've decided to go back?"

"You mean, go back home?"

"Are you sure it *is* home, still?"

"Oh dear—I'm not sure of anything—but—now Fred doesn't need me any more—will you tell me, Geo, what am I doing here?"

"You've got a lot of friends."

"Certainly I have. Friends. And they're real dears. The Peabodys and the Garfeins, especially, and Jerry and Flora, and I am very fond of Myrna Custer. But none of them *need* me. There isn't anyone who'd make me feel guilty about leaving them. . . . Now, Geo, be absolutely honest—is there anyone, *anyone at all*, I ought to feel guilty about leaving behind?"

There's me. No, he refuses to say it. Such flirting is unworthy of them, even when drunk. "Feeling guilty's no reason for staying *or* going," he tells her, firmly but kindly. "The point is, do you *want* to go? If you want to go, you should go. Never mind anybody else."

Charlotte nods sadly. "Yes, I suppose you're right."

George goes into the kitchen, fixes another round. (They seem to be drinking up much faster, now. This one really should be the last.) When he comes out again, she's sitting with her hands clasped, gazing in front of her. "I think I shall go back, Geo. I dread it—but I'm beginning to think I really shall."

"Why do you dread it?"

"In a way, I dread it. There's Nan, for one thing."

"You wouldn't have to live with her, would you?"

"I wouldn't have to. But I would. I'm sure I would."

"But, Charley—I've always had the impression that you loathe each other."

"Not *exactly* loathe. Anyhow, in a family, that's not really what matters. I mean, it can be beside the point. That's hard to explain to you, Geo, because you never had any family, did you, after you were quite young? No, I wouldn't say loathe. Though, of course, when I first got to know Buddy—when she found out we were sleeping together, that is—Nan did rather hate me. I mean, she hated my luck. Of course, in those days, Buddy *was* a dreamboat. Any sister might have felt jealous. But that wasn't the biggest part of it. What she really minded was that Buddy was a G.I. and that he was going to take me back to live in the States when we were married. Nan simply longed to come over here, you see—so many girls did, after wartime England and the shortages and everything—but she'd have died rather than admit it. She felt she was being disloyal to England even to want to come. I do believe she'd have far sooner admitted to being jealous of me with Buddy! Isn't that a laugh?"

"She knows you and Buddy have split up, of course?"

"Oh yes, I had to tell her at once, right after it happened. Otherwise, I'd have been so afraid she'd find out for herself, in some uncanny way, and that would have been too shaming. So I wrote to her about it, and she wrote back, such a beastly, quietly triumphing letter, saying Now I suppose you'll *have* to come back here—back to the country you deserted; that was what she implied. So of course I flew right off the handle—you know *me!*—and answered saying I was blissfully happy here, and that never never would I set foot on her dreary little island again. Oh, and then—I've never told you any of this, because it embarrassed me so—after I wrote *that* letter, I felt most terribly guilty, so I started sending her things: you know, delicatessen from those luxury shops in Beverly Hills, all sorts of cheeses and things in bottles and jars. As a matter of fact, living in this so-called land of plenty, I could hardly afford them! And I was such

140

an utter idiot, I didn't once stop to think how tactless I was being! Actually, I was playing right into Nan's hands. I mean, she let me go on sending all this stuff for a while—which she ate, I presume—and then *really* torpedoed me. Asked hadn't we heard in America that the war had been over quite some time, and that Bundles for Britain were out of date?"

"Charming creature!"

"No, Geo—underneath all that, Nan really loves me. It's just she wants me to see things her way. You know, she's two years older; that meant a lot when we were children. I've always thought of her as being sort of like a road—I mean, she *leads* somewhere. With her, I'll never lose my way. . . . Do you know what I'm trying to say?"

"No."

"Well, never mind. There's another thing about going back home—it's the past; and that's all tied up with Nan, too. Sort of going back to the place where I turned off the road, do you see?"

"No. I don't see."

"But, Geo—the *past!* Surely you can't pretend you don't know what I mean by that?"

"The past is just something that's over."

"Oh really—how *can* you be so tiresome!"

"No, Charley, I mean it. The past is over. People make believe that it isn't, and they show you things in museums. But that's not the past. You won't find the past in England. Or anywhere else, for that matter."

"Oh, you're tiresome!"

141

"Listen, why not just go back there on a visit? See Nan if you want to. But, for Christ's sake, don't commit yourself."

"No—if I go back at all, I've got to go back for good."

"*Why?*"

"I can't stand any more indecision. I've got to burn my boats, this time. I thought I'd done that when I came over here with Buddy. But, this time, I've got to—"

"Oh, for Christ's sake!"

"I know I'll find it all changed. I know there'll be a lot of things I'll hate. I know I'll miss all these supermarkets and labor-savers and conveniences. Probably I'll keep catching one cold after another, after living in this climate. And I expect you're quite right—I *shall* be miserable, living with Nan. I can't help any of that. At least, when I'm there, I shall know *where I am.*"

"Never in my born days have I heard such utter drooling masochism!"

"Oh yes, I know it sounds like that. And perhaps it is! Do you suppose masochism's our way of being patriotic? Or do I mean that the other way round? What fun! Darling, shouldn't we have another tiny drink? Let's drink to the masochism of Old England!"

"I don't think so, darling. Time for our beds."

"Geo—*you're leaving!*"

"I must, Charley."

"But when shall I see you?"

142

"Very soon. That is, unless you're taking off for England right away."

"Oh, don't tease me! You know perfectly well I'm not! It'd take me ages just to get ready. Perhaps I never will go at all. How could I ever face all that packing and the saying goodbye, and the *effort?* No —perhaps I never will—"

"We'll talk more about it. A lot more. . . . Good night, Charley dear."

She rises as he bends forward to kiss her. They bump awkwardly and very nearly topple over and roll on the floor. He steadies her, unsteadily.

"I should hate so to leave you, Geo."

"Then don't."

"The way you say that! I don't believe you care if I go or if I stay."

"Of course I care!"

"Truly?"

"Truly!"

"Geo?"

"Yes, Charley?"

"I don't think Jim would want me to leave you here alone."

"Then don't leave me."

"No—I'm dead serious! You remember when you and I drove up to San Francisco? In September, it must have been, last year, just after you got back from England—"

"Yes."

"Jim couldn't come up with us that day. I forget

143

why. He flew up the next day and joined us. Well, anyhow, just as you and I were getting into the car, Jim said something to me. Something I've never forgotten. . . . Did I ever tell you this?"

"I don't believe so." (She has told him at least six times; always when very drunk.)

"He said to me, You two take care of each other."

"He did?"

"Yes he did. Those were his exact words. And, Geo, I believe he didn't just mean take care. He meant something *more*—"

"What did he mean?"

"That was less than two months, wasn't it, before he left for Ohio. I believe he said *take care*, because he *knew*—"

Swaying a little, she regards him earnestly but dimly, as though she were peering up at him, fishlike, through all the liquor she has drunk. "Do *you* believe that, Geo?"

"How can we tell what he knew, Charley? As for our taking care of each other, we can be certain he'd have wanted us to do that." George puts his hands on her shoulders. "So now let's both tell each other to get some sleep, shall we?"

"No, wait—" She's like a child, stalling off bedtime with questions. "Do you suppose that pub is still for sale?"

"I expect so. That's an idea! Why don't we buy it, Charley? What do you say? We could get drunk and earn money at the same time. That'd be more fun than living with Nan!"

144

"Oh darling, how lovely! Do you suppose we really *could* buy it? No—you're not serious, are you? I can see you aren't. But don't ever say you aren't. Let's make plans about it, like you and Jim used to. He'd like us to make plans, wouldn't he?"

"Sure he would. . . . Good night, Charley."

"Goodnight, Geo, my love—" As they embrace, she kisses him full on the mouth. And suddenly sticks her tongue right in. She has done this before, often. It's one of those drunken long shots which just might, at least theoretically, once in ten thousand tries, throw a relationship right out of its orbit and send it whizzing off on another. Do women ever stop trying? No. But, because they never stop, they learn to be good losers. When, after a suitable pause, he begins to draw back, she doesn't attempt to cling to him. And now she accepts his going with no more resistance. He kisses her on the forehead. She is like a child who has at last submitted to being tucked into her cot.

"Sleep tight."

George turns, swings open the house door, takes one stride and—*oops!*—very very nearly falls head first down the steps—all of them—oh, and, unthinkably, much farther—ten, fifty, one hundred million feet into the bottomless black night. Only his grip on the door handle saves him.

He turns groggily, with a punching heart, to grin back at Charlotte; but luckily she has wandered away off somewhere. She hasn't seen him do this asinine thing. Which is truly providential because, if she *had* seen him, she would have insisted on his staying the

145

night; which would have meant, well, at the very least, such a late breakfast that it would have been brunch; which would have meant more drinks; which would have meant siesta and supper, and more and more and more drinks to follow. . . . This has actually happened, before now.

But this time he has escaped. And now he closes the house door with the care of a burglar, sits himself down on the top step, takes a deep breath, and gives himself a calm stern talking to. You are drunk. Oh, you stupid old thing, how dare you get so drunk? Well, now, listen: We are going to walk down those steps very slowly, and when we are at the bottom we are going straight home and upstairs and right into bed, without even brushing our teeth. All right, that's understood? Now, here we go. . . .

Well and good.

How to explain, then, that, with his foot actually on the bridge over the creek, George suddenly turns, chuckles to himself, and with the movement of a child wriggling free of a grownup—old guardian Cortex—runs off down the road, laughing, toward the ocean?

As he trots out of Camphor Tree Lane on to Las Ondas, he sees the round green porthole lights of The Starboard Side, down on the corner of the ocean highway across from the beach, shining to welcome him.

The Starboard Side has been here since the earliest days of the colony. Its bar, formerly a lunch counter, served the neighbors with their first post-prohibition beers, and the mirror behind it was sometimes honored by the reflection of Tom Mix. But its finest hours came later. That summer of 1945! The war as good as over. The blackout no more than an excuse for keeping the lights out at a gangbang. A sign over the bar said, "In case of a direct hit, we close immediately." Which was meant to be funny, of course. And yet, out across the bay, in deep water under the cliffs of Palos Verdes, lay a real Japanese submarine full of real dead Japanese, depth-bombed after they had sunk two or three ships in sight of the Californian coast.

You pushed aside the blackout curtain and elbowed your way through a jam-packed bar crowd, scarcely able to breathe or see for smoke. Here, in the complete privacy of the din and the crowd, you and your pickup yelled the preliminary sex advances at each other. You could flirt but you couldn't fight; there wasn't even room to smack someone's face. For that, you had to step outside. Oh, the bloody battles and the sidewalk vomitings! The punches flying wide, the heads crashing backwards against the fenders of parked cars! Huge diesel-dikes slugging it out, grimmer far than the men. The siren-wailing arrival of

147

the police; the sudden swoopings of the shore patrol. Girls dashing down from their apartments to drag some gorgeous endangered young drunk upstairs to safety and breakfast served next morning in bed like a miracle of joy. Hitch-hiking servicemen delayed at this corner for hours, nights, days; proceeding at last on their journey with black eyes, crab-lice, clap, and only the dimmest memory of their hostess or host.

And then the war's end and the mad spree of driving up and down the highway on the instantly de-rationed gas, shedding great black chunks of your recaps all the way to Malibu. And then the beach-months of 1946. The magic squalor of those hot nights, when the whole shore was alive with tongues of flame, the watchfires of a vast naked barbarian tribe—each group or pair to itself and bothering no one, yet all a part of the life of the tribal encamp-ment—swimming in the darkness, cooking fish, danc-ing to the radio, coupling without shame on the sand. George and Jim (who had just met) were out there among them evening after evening, yet not often enough to satisfy the sad fierce appetite of memory, as it looks back hungrily on that glorious Indian sum-mer of lust.

The hitch-hiking servicemen are few now and mostly domesticated, going back and forth between the rocket base and their homes and wives. Beach fires are forbidden, except in designated picnic areas where you must eat sitting up on benches at com-munal tables, and mustn't screw at all. But, though so much of the glory has faded, nevertheless—thanks

148

to the persecuted yet undying old gods of disorder—this last block of Las Ondas is still a bad neighborhood. Respectable people avoid it instinctively. Realtors deplore it. Property values are low here. The motels are new but cheaply stuck together and already slum-sordid; they cater to one-night stands. And, though the charcoal remnants of those barbarian orgy-fires have long since been ground into the sand, this stretch of the shore is still filthy with trash; high-school gangs still daub huge scandalous words on its beach-wall; and seashells are still less easy to find here than discarded rubbers.

The glory has faded, too, from The Starboard Side; only a true devotee like George can still detect even a last faint gleam of it. The place has been stripped of its dusty marine trophies and yellow group photographs. Right after the New Year it's to be what they dare to call redecorated: that's to say, desecrated, in readiness for next summer's mob of blank-faced strangers. Already there is a new juke-box; and a new television fixed high up on the wall, so you can turn half right, rest your elbow on the bar and go into a cow-daze, watching it. This is what most of the customers are doing, as George enters.

He makes unsteadily but purposefully for his favorite little table in the corner, from which the TV screen is invisible. At the table next to him, two other unhypnotized nonconformists, an elderly couple who belong to the last handful of surviving colonists, are practicing their way of love: a mild quarrelsome alcoholism which makes it possible for them to live in a

149

play-relationship, like children. *You old bag, you old prick, you old bitch, you old bastard:* rage without resentment, abuse without venom. This is how it will be for them till the end. Let's hope they will never be parted, but die in the same hour of the same night, in their beer-stained bed.

And now George's eyes move along the bar, stop on a figure seated alone at the end nearest the door. The young man isn't watching the TV; indeed, he is quite intent upon something he is writing on the back of an envelope. As he writes, he smiles to himself and rubs the side of his large nose with his forefinger. It is Kenny Potter.

At first, George doesn't move; seems hardly to react at all. But then a slow intent smile parts his lips. He leans forward, watching Kenny with the delight of a naturalist who has identified a rosy finch out of the high sierras on a tree in a city park. After a minute he rises, crosses almost stealthily to the bar and slips onto the stool beside Kenny.

"Hello, there," he says.

Kenny turns quickly, sees who it is, laughs loudly, crumples the envelope and tosses it over the bar into a trash container. "Hello, sir."

"What did you do that for?"

"Oh. Nothing."

"I disturbed you. You were writing."

"It was nothing. Only a poem."

"And now it's lost to the world!"

"I'll remember it. Now I've written it down."

"Would you say it for me?"

150

This sends Kenny into convulsions of laughter. "It's crazy. It's—" he gulps down his giggles—"it's a—a *haiku!*"

"Well, what's so crazy about a haiku?"

"I'd have to count the syllables first."

But Kenny obviously isn't going to count them now. So George says, "I didn't expect to see you in this neck of the woods. Don't you live over on the other side of town, near campus?"

"That's right. Only sometimes I like to get way away from there."

"But imagine your happening to pick on this particular bar!"

"Oh, that was because one of the kids told me you're in here a lot."

"You mean, you came out here to see me?" Perhaps George says this a little too eagerly. Anyhow, Kenny shrugs it off with a teasing smile.

"I thought I'd see what kind of a joint it was."

"It's nothing now. It used to be quite something, though. And I've gotten accustomed to coming here. You see, I live very close."

"Camphor Tree Lane?"

"How in the world did you know that?"

"Is it supposed to be a secret?"

"Why no—of course not! I have students come over to see me now and then. I mean, about their work—" George is immediately aware that this sounds defensive and guilty as hell. Has Kenny noticed? He is grinning; but then he has been grinning all the time. George adds, rather feebly, "You seem to know an awful lot about me and my habits. A lot more than I know about any of you—"

"There isn't much to know about us, I guess!" Kenny gives him a teasing, challenging look. "What would you like to know about us, sir?"

"Oh, I'll think of something. Give me time. Say, what are you drinking?"

"Nothing!" Kenny giggles. "He hasn't even noticed me yet." And, indeed, the bartender is absorbed in a TV wrestling match.

"Well, what'll you have?"

"What are you having, sir?"

"Scotch."

"Okay," Kenny says, in a tone which suggests that he would have agreed just as readily to buttermilk. George calls the bartender—very loudly, so he can't pretend not to have heard—and orders. The bartender, always a bit of a bitch, demands to see Kenny's I.D. So they go through all of that. George says stuffily to the bartender, "You ought to know me by this time. Do you really think I'd be such an idiot as to try to buy drinks for a minor?"

"We have to check," says the bartender, through a skin inches thick. He turns his back on them and moves away. George feels a brief spurt of powerless rage. He has been made to look like an ass—and in front of Kenny, too.

While they are waiting for the drinks, he asks, "How did you get here? In your car?"

"I don't have one. Lois drove me."

"Where is she now, then?"

"Gone home, I guess."

George senses something not quite in order. But, whatever it is, Kenny doesn't seem worried about it. He adds vaguely, "I thought I'd walk around for a while."

"But how'll you get back?"

"Oh, I'll manage."

(A voice inside George says, *You could invite him to stay the night at your place. Tell him you'll drive him back in the morning.* What in hell do you think I am? George asks it. *It was merely a suggestion,* says the voice.)

The drinks arrive. George says to Kenny, "Look, why don't we sit over there, at the table in the corner? That damned television keeps catching my eye."

"All right."

It *would* be fun, George thinks, if the young were just a little less passive. But that's too much to ask. You have to play it their way, or not at all. As they take their chairs, facing each other, George says, "I've still got my pencil sharpener," and, bringing it out of his pocket, he tosses it down on the table, as though shooting craps.

Kenny laughs. "I already lost mine!"

And now an hour, maybe, has passed. And they are both drunk: Kenny fairly, George very. But George is drunk in a good way, and one that he seldom achieves. He tries to describe to himself what this kind of drunkenness is like. Well—to put it very crudely—it's like Plato; it's a dialogue. A dialogue between two people. Yes, but not a Platonic dialogue in the hair-splitting, word-twisting, one-up-to-me sense; not a mock-humble bitching match; not a debate on some dreary set theme. You can talk about anything and change the subject as often as you like. In fact, what really matters is not what you talk about, but the being together in this particular relationship. George can't imagine having a dialogue of this kind with a woman, because women can only talk in terms of the personal. A man of his own age would do, if there was some sort of polarity; for instance, if he was a Negro. You and your dialogue-partner have to be somehow opposites. Why? Because you have to be symbolic figures—like, in this case, Youth and Age. Why do you have to be symbolic? Because the dialogue is by its nature impersonal. It's a symbolic encounter. It doesn't involve either party personally.

That's why, in a dialogue, you can say absolutely anything. Even the closest confidence, the deadliest secret, comes out objectively as a mere metaphor or illustration which could never be used against you.

George would like to explain all of this to Kenny. But it is so complicated, and he doesn't want to run the risk of finding that Kenny can't understand him. More than anything, he wants Kenny to understand, wants to be able to believe that Kenny knows what this dialogue is all about. And really, at this moment, it seems possible that Kenny *does* know. George can almost feel the electric field of the dialogue surrounding and irradiating them. *He* certainly feels irradiated. As for Kenny, he looks quite beautiful. *Radiant with rapport* is the phrase which George finds to describe him. For what shines out of Kenny isn't mere intelligence or any kind of switched-on charm. There the two of them sit, smiling at each other—oh, far more than that—fairly beaming with mutual insight.

"Say something," he commands Kenny.

"Do I have to?"

"Yes."

"What'll I say?"

"Anything. Anything that seems to be important, right now."

"That's the trouble. I don't know what is important and what isn't. I feel like my head is stopped up with stuff that doesn't matter—I mean, matter to me."

"Such as—"

"Look, I don't mean to be personal, sir—but—well, the stuff our classes are about—"

155

"That doesn't matter to you?"

"Jesus Christ, sir—I *said* I wasn't being personal! Yours are a whole lot better than most; we all think that. And you do try to make these books fit in with what's going on nowadays, only, it's not your fault, but—we always seem to end up getting bogged down in the past; like this morning, with Tithonus. Look, I don't want to pan the past; maybe it'll mean a whole lot to me when I'm older. All I'm saying is, the past doesn't really matter to most kids my age. When we talk like it does, we're just being polite. I guess that's because we don't have any pasts of our own—except stuff we want to forget, like things in high school, and times we acted like idiots—"

"Well, fine! I can understand that. You don't need the past, yet. You've got the present."

"Oh, but the present's a real drag! I just despise the present—I mean, the way it is right now—I mean, tonight's an exception, of course— What are you laughing at, sir?"

"Tonight—*sí!* The present—*no!*" George is getting noisy. Some people at the bar turn their heads. "Drink to tonight!" He drinks, with a flourish.

"Tonight—*sí!*" Kenny laughs and drinks.

"Okay," says George. "The past—no help. The present—no good. Granted. But there's one thing you can't deny; you're stuck with the future. You can't just sneeze that off."

"I guess we are. What's left of it. There may not be much, with all these rockets—"

"Death."

156

"Death?"

"That's what I said."

"Come again, sir. I don't get you."

"I said death. I said, do you think about death a lot?"

"Why, no. Hardly at all. Why?"

"The future—that's where death is."

"Oh—yeah. Yeah—maybe you've got a point there." Kenny grins. "You know something? Maybe the other generations before us used to think about death a lot more than we do. What I mean is, kids must have gotten mad, thinking how they'd be sent out to some corny war and killed, while their folks stayed home and acted patriotic. But it won't be like that any more. We'd all be in this thing together."

"You could still get mad at the older people. Because of all those extra years they'll have had before they get blown up."

"Yes, that's right, I could, couldn't I? Maybe I will. Maybe I'll get mad at you, sir."

"Kenneth—"

"Sir?"

"Just as a matter of the purest sociological interest, why do you persist in calling me sir?"

Kenny grins teasingly. "I'll stop if you want me to."

"I didn't ask you to stop. I asked you why."

"Why don't you like it? None of you do, though, I guess."

"You mean, none of us old folks?" George smiles a no-hard-feelings smile. Nevertheless, he feels that the symbolic relationship is starting to get out of hand.

157

"Well, the usual explanation is that we don't like being reminded—"

Kenny shakes his head decisively. "No."

"What do you mean, 'No'?"

"You're not like that."

"Is that supposed to be a compliment?"

"Maybe. The point is, I *like* calling you sir."

"You do?"

"What's so phony nowadays is all this familiarity. Pretending there isn't any difference between people —well, like you were saying about minorities, this morning. If you and I are no different, what do we have to give each other? How can we ever be friends?"

He *does* understand, George thinks, delighted. "But two young people can be friends, surely?"

"That's something else again. They can, yes, after a fashion. But there's always this thing of competition, getting in the way. All young people are kind of competing with each other, do you know that?"

"Yes, I suppose so—unless they're in love."

"Maybe they are even then. Maybe that's what's wrong with—" Kenny breaks off abruptly. George watches him, expecting to hear some confidence about Lois. But it doesn't come. For Kenny is obviously following some quite different train of thought. He sits smiling in silence for a few moments and— yes, actually—he is blushing! "This sounds as corny as hell, but—"

"Never mind. Go ahead."

"I sometimes wish—I mean, when you read those

158

Victorian novels—I'd have hated living in those days, all except for one thing—oh, hell—I can't say it!" He breaks off, blushing and laughing.

"Don't be silly!"

"When I say it, it's so corny, it's the end! But—I'd have liked living when you could call your father sir."

"Is your father alive?"

"Oh, sure."

"Why don't you call him sir, then? Some sons do, even nowadays."

"Not my father. He isn't the type. Besides, he isn't around. He ran out on us a couple of years ago. . . . Hell!"

"What's the matter?"

"Whatever made me tell you all that? Am I drunk or something?"

"No more drunk than I am."

"I must be stoned."

"Look—if it bothers you—let's forget you told me."

"*I* won't forget."

"Oh yes, you will. You'll forget if I tell you to forget."

"Will I?"

"You bet you will!"

"Well, if you say so—okay."

"Okay, *sir*."

"Okay, *sir!*" Kenny suddenly beams. He is really pleased—so pleased that his own pleasure embarrasses him. "Say, you know—when I came over here—I mean, when I thought I might just happen to run into you this evening—there was something I wanted to ask you. I just remembered what it was—" he downs the rest of his drink in one long swallow—"it's about experience. They keep telling you, when you're older, you'll have experience—and that's supposed to be so great. What would you say about that, sir? Is it really any use, would you say?"

"What kind of experience?"

"Well—places you've been to, people you've met. Situations you've been through already, so you know how to handle them when they come up again. All that stuff that's supposed to make you wise, in your later years."

"Let me tell you something, Kenny. For other people, I can't speak—but, personally, I haven't gotten wise on anything. Certainly, I've been through this and that; and when it happens again, I say to myself, Here it is again. But that doesn't seem to help me. In my opinion, I, personally, have gotten steadily sillier and sillier and sillier—and that's a fact."

"No kidding, sir? You can't mean that! You mean, sillier than when you were young?"

"Much, much sillier."

"I'll be darned. Then experience is no use at all? You're saying it might just as well not have happened?"

"No. I'm not saying that. I only mean, you can't *use* it. But if you don't try to—if you just realize it's there and you've got it—then it can be kind of marvelous."

"Let's go swimming," says Kenny abruptly, as if bored by the whole conversation.

160

"All right."

Kenny throws his head right back and laughs wildly. "Oh—that's terrific!"

"What's terrific?"

"It was a test. I thought you were bluffing, about being silly. So I said to myself, I'll suggest doing something wild, and if he objects—if he even hesitates—then I'll know it was all a bluff. You don't mind my telling you that, do you, sir?"

"Why should I?"

"Oh, that's terrific!"

"Well, I'm not bluffing—so what are we waiting for? *You* weren't bluffing, were you?"

"Hell, no!"

They jump up, pay, run out of the bar and across the highway, and Kenny vaults the railing and drops down, about eight feet, onto the beach. George, meanwhile, is clambering over the rail, a bit stiffly. Kenny looks up, his face still lit by the boardwalk lamps: "Put your feet on my shoulders, sir." George does so, drunk-trustful, and Kenny, with the deftness of a ballet dancer, supports him by ankles and calves, lowering him almost instantly to the sand. During the descent, their bodies rub against each other, briefly but roughly. The electric field of the dialogue is broken. Their relationship, whatever it now is, is no longer symbolic. They turn and begin to run toward the ocean.

Already the lights seem far, far behind. They are bright but they cast no beams; perhaps they are shining on a layer of high fog. The waves ahead are barely

161

visible. Their blackness is immensely cold and wet. Kenny is tearing off his clothes with wild whooping cries. The last remaining minim of George's caution is aware of the lights and the possibility of cruise cars and cops, but he doesn't hesitate, he is no longer able to; this dash from the bar can only end in the water. He strips himself clumsily, tripping over his pants. Kenny, stark naked now, has plunged and is wading straight in, like a fearless native warrior, to attack the waves. The undertow is very strong. George flounders for a while in a surge of stones. As he finally struggles through and feels sand under his feet, Kenny comes body-surfing out of the night and shoots past him without a glance—a water-creature absorbed in its element.

As for George, these waves are much too big for him. They seem truly tremendous, towering up, blackness unrolling itself out of blackness, mysteriously and awfully sparkling, then curling over in a thundering slap of foam which is sparked with phosphorus. George has sparks of it all over his body, and he laughs with delight to find himself bejeweled. Laughing, gasping, choking, he is too drunk to be afraid; the salt water he swallows seems as intoxicating as whiskey. From time to time he catches tremendous glimpses of Kenny, arrowing down some toppling foam-precipice. Then, intent upon his own rites of purification, George staggers out once more, wide-open-armed, to receive the stunning baptism of the surf. Giving himself to it utterly, he washes away thought, speech, mood, desire, whole selves, entire

162

lifetimes; again and again he returns, becoming always cleaner, freer, less. He is perfectly happy by himself; it's enough to know that Kenny and he are the sole sharers of the element. The waves and the night and the noise exist only for their play. Meanwhile, no more than two hundred yards distant, the lights shine from the shore and the cars flick past up and down the highway, flashing their long beams. On the dark hillsides you can see lamps in the windows of dry homes, where the dry are going dryly to their dry beds. But George and Kenny are refugees from dryness; they have escaped across the border into the water-world, leaving their clothes behind them for a customs fee.

And now, suddenly, here is a great, an apocalyptically great wave, and George is way out, almost out of his depth, standing naked and tiny before its presence, under the lip of its roaring upheaval and the towering menace of its fall. He tries to dive through it—even now he feels no real fear—but instead he is caught and picked up, turned over and over and over, flapping and kicking toward a surface which may be either up or down or sideways, he no longer knows.

And now Kenny is dragging him out, groggy-legged. Kenny's hands are under George's armpits and he is laughing and saying like a nanny, "That's enough for now!" And George, still water-drunk, gasps, "I'm all right," and wants to go straight back into the water. But Kenny says, "Well, *I'm* not—I'm cold," and nannylike he towels George, with his own shirt, not George's, until George stops him because

163

his back is sore. The nanny-relationship is so convincing at this moment that George feels he could curl up and fall immediately asleep right here, shrunk to child-size within the safety of Kenny's bigness. Kenny's body seems to have grown gigantic since they left the water. Everything about him is larger than life: the white teeth of his grin, the wide dripping shoulders, the tall slim torso with its heavy-hung sex, and the long legs, now beginning to shiver.

"Can we go back to your place, sir?" he asks.

"Sure. Where else?"

"Where else?" Kenny repeats, seeming to find this very amusing. He picks up his clothes and turns, still naked, toward the highway and the lights.

"Are you crazy?" George shouts after him.

"What's the matter?" Kenny looks back, grinning.

"You're going to walk home like that? Are you crazy? They'd call the cops!"

Kenny shrugs his shoulders good-humoredly. "Nobody would have seen us. We're invisible—didn't you know?"

But he gets into his clothes now, and George does likewise. As they start up the beach again, Kenny puts his arm around George's shoulder. "You know something, sir? They ought not to let you out on your own, ever. You're liable to get into real trouble."

Their walk home sobers George quite a lot. By the time they reach the house, he no longer sees the two of them as wild water-creatures but as an elderly professor with wet hair bringing home an exceedingly wet student in the middle of the night. George becomes self-conscious and almost curt. "The bathroom's upstairs. I'll get you some towels."

Kenny reacts to the formality at once. "Aren't you taking a shower too, sir?" he asks, in a deferential, slightly disappointed tone.

"I can do that later. I wish I had some clothes your size to lend you. You'll have to wrap up in a blanket, while we dry your things on the heater. It's rather a slow process, I'm afraid, but that's the best we can do."

"Look, sir—I don't want to be a nuisance. Why don't I go now?"

"Don't be an idiot. You'd get pneumonia."

"My clothes'll dry on me. I'll be all right."

"Nonsense! Come on up and I'll show you where everything is."

George's refusal to let him leave appears to have

165

pleased Kenny. At any rate, he makes a terrific noise in the shower, not so much singing as a series of shouts. He is probably waking up the neighbors, George thinks, but who cares? George's spirits are up again; he feels excited, amused, alive. In his bedroom, he undresses quickly, gets into his thick white terry-cloth bathrobe, hurries downstairs again, puts on the kettle and fixes some tuna fish and tomato sandwiches on rye. They are all ready, set out on a tray in the living room when Kenny comes down, wearing the blanket awkwardly, saved-from-shipwreck style.

Kenny doesn't want coffee or tea; he would rather have beer, he says. So George gets him a can from the icebox and unwisely pours himself a biggish Scotch. He returns to find Kenny looking around the room as though it fascinates him.

"You live here all by yourself, sir?"

"Yes," says George, and adds with a shade of irony, "Does that surprise you?"

"No. One of the kids said he thought you did."

"As a matter of fact, I used to share this place with a friend."

But Kenny shows no curiosity about the friend. "You don't even have a cat or a dog or anything?"

"You think I should?" George asks, a bit aggressive. The poor old guy doesn't have anything to love, he thinks Kenny is thinking.

"Hell, no! Didn't Baudelaire say they're liable to turn into demons and take over your life?"

"Something like that. This friend of mine had lots

166

of animals, though, and they didn't seem to take *us* over. Of course, it's different when there's two of you. We often used to agree that neither one of us would want to keep on the animals if the other wasn't there. . . ."

No. Kenny is absolutely not curious about any of this. Indeed, he is concentrating on taking a huge bite out of his sandwich. So George asks him, "Is it all right?"

"I'll say!" He grins at George with his mouth full, then swallows and adds, "You know something, sir? I believe you've discovered the secret of the perfect life!"

"I have?" George has just gulped nearly a quarter of his Scotch to drown out a spasm which started when he talked about Jim and the animals. Now he feels the alcohol coming back on him with a rush. It is exhilarating, but it is coming much too fast.

"You don't realize how many kids my age just dream about the kind of setup you've got here. I mean, what more can you want? I mean, you don't have to take orders from anybody. You can do any crazy thing that comes into your head."

"And that's your idea of the perfect life?"

"Sure it is!"

"Honestly?"

"What's the matter, sir? Don't you believe me?"

"What I don't quite understand is, if you're so keen on living alone—how does Lois fit in?"

"Lois? What's she got to do with it?"

"Now, look, Kenny—I don't mean to be nosy—but,

167

rightly or wrongly, I got the idea that you and she might be, well, considering—"

"Getting married? No. That's out."

"Oh?"

"She says she won't marry a Caucasian. She says she can't take people in this country seriously. She doesn't feel anything we do here *means* anything. She wants to go back to Japan and teach."

"She's an American citizen, isn't she?"

"Oh, sure. She's a Nisei. But, just the same, she and her whole family got shipped up to one of those internment camps in the Sierras, right after the war began. Her father had to sell his business for peanuts, give it away, practically, to some sharks who were grabbing all the Japanese property and talking big about avenging Pearl Harbor! Lois was only a small kid, then, but you can't expect anyone to forget a thing like that. She says they were all treated as enemy aliens; no one even gave a damn which side they were on. She says the Negroes were the only ones who acted decently to them. And a few pacifists. Christ, she certainly has the right to hate our guts! Not that she does, actually. She always seems to be able to see the funny side of things."

"And how do you feel about her?"

"Oh, I like her a lot."

"And she likes you, doesn't she?"

"I guess so. Yes, she does. A lot."

"But don't you *want* to marry her?"

"Oh sure. I guess so. If she were to change her attitude. But I doubt if she will. And, anyhow, I'm in no rush about marrying anyone. There's a lot of things I want to do, first—" Kenny pauses, regarding George with his most teasing, penetrating grin. "You know what I think, sir?"

"What do you think?"

"I don't believe you're that much interested whether I marry Lois or not. I think you want to ask me something different. Only you're not sure how I'll take it."

"What do I want to ask you?"

This is getting positively flirty, on both sides. Kenny's blanket, under the relaxing influence of the talk and beer, has slipped, baring an arm and a shoulder and turning itself into a classical Greek garment, the chlamys worn by a young disciple—the favorite, surely—of some philosopher. At this moment, he is utterly, dangerously charming.

"You want to know if Lois and I—if we make out together."

"Well, do you?"

Kenny laughs triumphantly. "So I was right!"

"Maybe. Maybe not. . . . Do you?"

"We did, once."

"Why only once?"

"It wasn't so long ago. We went to a motel. It's down the beach, as a matter of fact, quite near here."

"Is that why you drove out here tonight?"

"Yes—partly. I was trying to talk her into going there again."

"And that's what the argument was about?"

"Who says we had an argument?"

169

"You left her to drive home alone, didn't you?"

"Oh well, that was because. . . . No, you're right —she didn't want to. She hated that motel the first time, and I don't blame her. The office and the desk clerk and the register—all that stuff they put you through. And of course they know damn well what the score is. It all makes the thing much too important and corny, like some big sin or something. And the way they look at you! Girls mind all that much more than we do—"

"So now she's called the whole thing off?"

"Hell, no, it's not that bad! It's not that she's against it, you understand. Not on principle. In fact, she's definitely—well, anyhow, I guess we can work something out. We'll have to see. . . ."

"You mean, maybe you can find some place that isn't so public and embarrassing?"

"That'd be a big help, certainly." Kenny grins, yawns, stretches himself. The chlamys slips off his other shoulder. He pulls it back over both shoulders as he rises, turning it into a blanket again and himself into a gawky twentieth-century American boy comically stranded without his clothes. "Look, sir, it's getting as late as all hell. I have to be going."

"Where, may I ask?"

"Why, back across town."

"In what?"

"I can get a bus, can't I?"

"They won't start running for another two hours, at least."

"Just the same . . ."

"Why don't you stay here? Tomorrow I'll drive you."

"I don't think I . . ."

"If you start wandering around this neighborhood in the dark, now the bars are shut, the police will stop you and ask what you're doing. And you aren't exactly sober, if you don't mind my saying so. They might even take you in."

"Honestly, sir, I'll be all right."

"I think you're out of your mind. However, we'll discuss that in a minute. First—sit down. I've got something I want to tell you."

Kenny sits down obediently, without further protest. Perhaps he is curious to know what George's next move will be.

"Now listen to this very carefully. I am about to make a simple statement of fact. Or facts. No comment is required from you. If you like, you can decide that this doesn't concern you at all. Is that clear?"

"Yes, sir."

"There's a woman I know who lives near here—a very close friend of mine. We have supper together at least one day a week; often, more than that. Matter of fact, we had supper tonight. Now—it never makes any difference to her which day I pick. So what I've decided is this—and, mind, it has nothing whatsoever to do with you, *necessarily*—from now on, I shall go to her place for supper each week on the same night. *Invariably, on the same night.* Tonight, that is. Is that much clear? No, don't answer. Go right on listening, because I'm just coming to the point. These nights, when I have supper with my friend, *I shall never, under any circumstances*, return here before midnight. Is that clear? No—listen! This house is never locked, because anyone could get into it anyway just by breaking a panel in the glass door. Upstairs, in my study, you must have noticed that there's a couch bed? I keep it made up with clean sheets on it, just on the once-in-a-blue-moon chance that I'll get an unexpected guest—such as you are going to be tonight, for instance. . . . No—listen carefully! If that bed were ever used while I was out, and straightened up afterwards, I'd never be any the wiser. And if my cleaning woman were to notice anything, she'd merely put the sheets out to go to the laundry; she'd suppose I'd had a guest and forgotten to tell her. . . . All right! I've made a decision and now I've told you about it. Just as I might tell you I'd decided to water the garden on a certain day of the week. I have also told you a few facts about this house. You can make a note of them. Or you can forget them. That's all."

George looks straight at Kenny. Kenny smiles back at him faintly. But he is—yes, just a little bit—embarrassed.

"And now get me another drink."

"Okay, sir." Kenny rises from his chair with noticeable eagerness, as if glad of this breaking of tension. He picks up George's glass and goes into the kitchen. George calls after him, "And get yourself one, too!"

172

Kenny puts his head around the corner, grinning. "Is that an order, sir?"

"You're damn right it is!"

I suppose you've decided I'm a dirty old man?"

While Kenny was getting the drinks from the kitchen, George felt himself entering a new phase. Now, as Kenny takes his seat again, he is, though he cannot have realized it yet, in the presence of a George transformed: a formidable George, who articulates thickly but clearly, with a menace behind his words. An inquisitorial George, seated in judgment and perhaps about to pronounce sentence. An oracular George, who may shortly begin to speak with tongues.

This isn't at all like their drunkenness at The Starboard Side. Kenny and he are no longer in the symbolic dialogue-relationship; this new phase of communication is very much person-to-person. Yet, paradoxically, Kenny seems farther away, not closer; he has receded far beyond the possible limits of an electric field. Indeed, it is only now and then that George

173

can see him clearly, for the room has become dazzlingly bright, and Kenny's face keeps fading into the
brightness. Also, there is a loud buzzing in George's
ears, so loud that he can't be certain if Kenny answered his question or not.

"You needn't say anything," George tells Kenny
(thus dealing with either possibility), "because I
admit it—oh, hell, yes, of course I admit it—I *am* a
dirty old man. Ninety-nine per cent of all old men are
dirty. That is, if you want to talk that language; if
you insist on that kind of dreariness. I'm not protesting against what you choose to call me or don't. I'm
protesting against an attitude—and I'm only doing
that for your sake, not mine. . . .

"Look—things are quite bad enough anyhow, nowadays—we're in quite enough of a mess, semantically
and every other way—without getting ourselves en-
tangled in these dreary categories. I mean, what is
this life of ours supposed to be *for?* Are we to spend
it identifying each other with catalogues, like tourists
in an art gallery? Or are we to try to exchange *some*
kind of a signal, however garbled, before it's too late?
You answer *me* that!

"It's all very fine and easy for you young things to
come to me on campus and tell me I'm cagey. Merci-
ful Christ—*cagey!* Don't you even know better than
that? Don't you have a glimmering of how I must feel
—longing to *speak?*

"You asked me about experience. So I told you.
Experience isn't any *use*. And yet, in quite another
way, it *might* be. If only we weren't all such miserable

174

fools and prudes and cowards. Yes, you too, my boy. And don't you dare deny it! What I said just now, about the bed in the study—that shocked you. Because you were determined to be shocked. You utterly refused to understand my motives. Oh God, don't you *see?* That bed—what that bed *means*—that's what experience *is!*

"Oh well, I'm not blaming you. It'd be a miracle if you *did* understand. Never mind. Forget it. Here am I. Here are you—in that damned blanket. Why don't you take it right off, for Christ's sake? What made me say that? I suppose you're going to misunderstand that, too? Well, if you do, I don't give a damn. The point is—here am I and here are you—and for once there's no one to disturb us. This may never happen again. I mean that literally! And the time is *desperately* short. All right, let's put the cards on the table. Why are you here in this room at this moment? *Because you want me to tell you something!* That's the true reason you came all the way across town tonight. You may have honestly believed it was to get Lois in bed with you. Mind you, I'm not saying one word against her. She's a truly beautiful angel. But you can't fool a dirty old man; he isn't sentimental about Young Love; he knows just how much it's worth—a great deal, but not everything. No, my dear Kenneth. You came here this evening to see *me*—whether you realize it or not. Some part of you knew quite well that Lois would refuse to go to that motel again; and that that would give you an excuse to send her home and get yourself stranded out here. I expect that poor

175

girl is feeling terrible about it all, right now, and crying into her pillow. You must be very sweet to her when you see her again. . . .

"But I'm getting off the point. The point is, you came to ask me about something that really *is* important. So why be ashamed and deny it? You see, I know you through and through. I know *exactly* what you want. You want me to tell you *what I know.*

"Oh, Kenneth, Kenneth, believe me—there's nothing I'd rather do! I want *like hell* to tell you. But I can't. I quite literally can't. Because, don't you see, *what I know is what I am?* And I can't tell you that. You have to find it out for yourself. I'm like a book you have to read. A book can't read itself to you. It doesn't even know what it's about. I don't know what I'm about.

"You could know what I'm about. You could. But you can't be bothered to. Look—you're the only boy I ever met on that campus I really believe could. That's what makes it so tragically futile. Instead of trying to know, you commit the inexcusable triviality of saying 'he's a dirty old man,' and turning this evening, which might be the most precious and unforgettable of your young life, into a *flirtation!* You don't like that word, do you? But it's the word. It's the enormous tragedy of everything nowadays: flirtation. Flirtation instead of fucking, if you'll pardon my coarseness. All any of you ever do is flirt, and wear your blankets off one shoulder, and complain about motels. And miss the one thing that might really—

176

and, Kenneth, I do not say this casually—*transform your entire life—*"

For a moment, Kenny's face is quite distinct. It grins, dazzlingly. Then his grin breaks up, is refracted, or whatever you call it, into rainbows of light. The rainbows blaze. George is blinded by them. He shuts his eyes. And now the buzzing in his ears is the roar of Niagara.

Half an hour, an hour, later—not long, anyway—George blinks and is awake.

Night, still. Dark. Warm. Bed. *Am in bed!* He jerks up, propped on his elbow. Clicks on the bedside lamp. His hand does this; arm in sleeve; pajama sleeve. *Am in pajamas!* Why? How?

Where is he?

George staggers out of bed, dizzy, a bit sickish, startled wide awake. Ready to lurch into the front room. No—wait. Here's paper propped against lamp:

Thought maybe I'd better split, after all. I like to wander around at night. If those cops pick me up, I won't tell them where I've been—I promise! Not even if they twist my arm!

That was great, this evening. Let's do it again, shall we? Or don't you believe in repeating things?

Couldn't find pajamas you already used, so took these clean ones from the drawer. Maybe you sleep raw? Didn't want to take a chance, though. Can't have you getting pneumonia, can we?

Thanks for everything,

Kenneth

George sits on the bed, reading this. Then, with slight impatience, like a general who has just glanced through an unimportant dispatch, he lets the paper slide to the floor, stands up, goes into the bathroom, empties his bladder, doesn't glance in the mirror, doesn't even turn on the light, returns to bed, gets in, switches off bed lamp.

Little teaser, his mind says, but without the least resentment. Just as well he didn't stay.

But, as he lies on his back in the dark, there is something that keeps him from sleep: a tickle in the blood and the nerves of the groin. The alcohol itches in him, down there.

Lying in the dark, he conjures up Kenny and Lois in their car, makes them drive into Camphor Tree Lane, park further down the street, in case a neighbor should be watching, hurry discreetly across the bridge, get the door open—it sticks, she giggles—bump against the living-room furniture—a tiny Japanese cry of alarm—tiptoe upstairs without turning on the lights. . . .

No—it won't work. George tries several times, but he just cannot make Lois go up those stairs. Each time he starts her up them, she dematerializes, as it were. (And now he knows, with absolute certainty, that Kenny will never be able to persuade her even to enter this house.)

But the play has begun, now, and George isn't about to stop it. Kenny must be provided with a partner. So George turns Lois into the sexy little gold cat, the Mexican tennis player. No trouble about getting *him* upstairs! He and Kenny are together in the front room, now. George hears a belt drop to the floor. They are stripping themselves naked.

The blood throbs deep down in George's groin. The flesh stirs and swells up, suddenly hard hot. The pajamas are pulled off, tossed out of bed.

George hears Kenny whisper to the Mexican, *Come on, kid!* Making himself invisible, he enters the front room. He finds the two of them just about to lie down together. . . .

No. That won't work, either. George doesn't like Kenny's attitude. He isn't taking his lust seriously; in fact, he seems to be on the verge of giggles. Quick— we need a substitute! George hastily turns Kenny into the big blond boy from the tennis court. Oh, much better! Perfect! Now they can embrace. Now the fierce hot animal play can begin. George hovers above them, watching; then he begins passing in and out of

179

their writhing, panting bodies. He is either. He is both at once. Ah—it is so good! Ah—ah . . . !

You old idiot, George's mind says. But he is not ashamed of himself. He speaks to the now slack and sweating body with tolerant good humor, as if to an old greedy dog which has just gobbled down a chunk of meat far bigger than it really wanted. Well, maybe you'll let us sleep, now? His hand feels for a handkerchief from under the pillow, wipes his belly dry.

As sleep begins to wash lightly over him, he asks himself, Shall I mind meeting Kenny's eye in class on Monday?

No. Not a bit. Even if he has told Lois (which I doubt): I undressed him, I put him to bed, he was drunk as a skunk. For then he will have told her about the swimming, too: You should have seen him in that water—as crazy as a kid! They ought not to let you out on your own, I said to him.

George smiles to himself, with entire self-satisfaction. Yes, I *am* crazy, he thinks. That is my secret; my strength.

And I'm about to get much crazier, he announces. Just watch me, all of you! Do you know what? I'm flying to Mexico for Christmas! You dare me to? I'll make reservations first thing in the morning!

He falls asleep, still smiling.

Partial surfacings, after this. Partial emergings, just barely breaking the sheeted calm of the water. Most of George remaining submerged in sleep.

Just barely awash, the brain inside its skull on the pillow cognizes darkly; not in its daytime manner. It is incapable of decision now. But, perhaps for this very reason, it can become aware, in this state, of certain decisions apparently not yet made. Decisions that are like codicils which have been secretly signed and witnessed and put away in a most private place to await the hour of their execution.

Daytime George may even question the maker of these decisions; but he will not be allowed to remember its answers in the morning.

What if Kenny has been scared off? What if he doesn't come back? Let him stay away. George doesn't need him, or any of these kids. He isn't looking for a son.

What if Charlotte goes back to England?

He can do without her, if he must. He doesn't need a sister.

Will George go back to England?

No. He will stay here.

Because of Jim?

No. Jim is in the past, now. He is of no use to George any more.

But George remembers him so faithfully.

George makes himself remember. He is afraid of forgetting. Jim is my life, he says. But he will have to forget, if he wants to go on living. Jim is death.

Then why will George stay here?

This is where he found Jim. He believes he will find another Jim here. He doesn't know it, but he has started looking already.

Why does George believe he will find him?

He only knows that he must find him. He believes he will because he must.

But George is getting old. Won't it very soon be too late?

Never use those words to George. He won't listen. He daren't listen. Damn the future. Let Kenny and the kids have it. Let Charley keep the past. George clings only to Now. It is Now that he must find another Jim. Now that he must love. Now that he must live. . . .

182

Meanwhile, here we have this body known as George's body, asleep on this bed and snoring quite loud. The dampness of the ocean air affects its sinuses; and anyhow, it snores extra loud after drinking. Jim used to kick it awake, turn it over on its side, sometimes get out of bed in a fury and go to sleep in the front room.

But *is* all of George altogether present here?

Up the coast a few miles north, in a lava reef under the cliffs, there are a lot of rock pools. You can visit them when the tide is out. Each pool is separate and different, and you can, if you are fanciful, give them names, such as George, Charlotte, Kenny, Mrs. Strunk. Just as George and the others are thought of, for convenience, as individual entities, so you may think of a rock pool as an entity; though, of course, it is not. The waters of its consciousness—so to speak—are swarming with hunted anxieties, grim-jawed greeds, dartingly vivid intuitions, old crusty-shelled rock-gripping obstinacies, deep-down sparkling undiscovered secrets, ominous protean organisms motioning mysteriously, perhaps warningly, toward the surface light. How can such a variety of creatures co-exist at all? Because they have to. The rocks of the pool hold their world together. And, throughout the day of the ebb tide, they know no other.

But that long day ends at last; yields to the night-time of the flood. And, just as the waters of the ocean come flooding, darkening over the pools, so over George and the others in sleep come the waters of that other ocean—that consciousness which is no one in particular but which contains everyone and every-thing, past, present and future, and extends unbroken beyond the uttermost stars. We may surely suppose that, in the darkness of the full flood, some of these creatures are lifted from their pools to drift far out over the deep waters. But do they ever bring back, when the daytime of the ebb returns, any kind of catch with them? Can they tell us, in any manner, about their journey? Is there, indeed, anything for them to tell—except that the waters of the ocean are not really other than the waters of the pool?

W ithin this body on the bed, the great pump works on and on, needing no rest. All over this quietly pulsating vehicle the skeleton crew make their tiny adjustments. As for what goes on topside, they know nothing of this but danger signals, false alarms mostly: red lights flashed from the panicky brain stem, curtly contradicted by green all clears from the level-headed cortex. But now the controls are on automatic. The cortex is drowsing; the brain stem registers only an occasional nightmare. Everything seems set for a routine run from here to morning. The odds are enormously against any kind of accident. The safety record of this vehicle is outstanding.

Just let us suppose, however. . . .

Let us take the particular instant, years ago, when George walked into The Starboard Side and set eyes for the first time on Jim, not yet demobilized and looking stunning beyond words in his Navy uniform. Let us then suppose that, at that same instant, deep down in one of the major branches of George's coronary artery, an unimaginably gradual process began. Somehow—no doctor can tell us exactly why—the inner lining begins to become roughened. And, one by one, on the roughened surface of the smooth endothelium, ions of calcium, carried by the bloodstream, begin to be deposited. . . . Thus, slowly, invisibly, with the utmost discretion and without the slightest hint to those old fussers in the brain, an almost indecently melodramatic situation is contrived: the formation of the atheromatous plaque.

Let us suppose this, merely. (The body on the bed is still snoring.) This thing is wildly improbable. You could bet thousands of dollars against its happening,

185

tonight or any night. And yet it *could,* quite possibly, be about to happen—within the next five minutes.

Very well—let us suppose that this is the night, and the hour, and the appointed minute.

Now—

The body on the bed stirs slightly, perhaps; but it does not cry out, does not wake. It shows no outward sign of the instant, annihilating shock. Cortex and brain stem are murdered in the blackout with the speed of an Indian strangler. Throttled out of its oxygen, the heart clenches and stops. The lungs go dead, their power line cut. All over the body, the arterials contract. Had this blockage not been absolute, had the occlusion occurred in one of the smaller branches of the artery, the skeleton crew could have dealt with it; they are capable of engineering miracles. Given time, they could have rigged up bypasses, channeled out new collateral communications, sealed off the damaged area with a scar. But there is no time at all. They die without warning at their posts.

For a few minutes, maybe, life lingers in the tissues of some outlying regions of the body. Then, one by one, the lights go out and there is total blackness. And if some part of the nonentity we called George has indeed been absent at this moment of terminal shock, away out there on the deep waters, then it will return to find itself homeless. For it can associate no longer with what lies here, unsnoring, on the bed. This is now cousin to the garbage in the container on the back porch. Both will have to be carted away and disposed of, before too long.